Family Happiness
Stories by
Jon Sindell

ISBN: 978-0-9965405-3-7

Printed in the United States of America

Cover Design: Jon Sindell
Front Cover Photo: Jon Sindell

Also by Jon Sindell:
The Roadkill Collection
The Mighty Roman Baseball Blast

BIG TABLE Publishing
Big Table Publishing Company
Boston, MA
www.bigtablepublishing.com

For my grandfather, Abraham Chapman—an oak in the family grove.

Acknowledgments

I would like to express my deep gratitude to: my family, especially my infinitely supportive wife, Kathy; the editors who gave many of these stories their first home; Deborah Steinberg, for her wise advice; the authors Christopher Bundy, Stephen D. Gutierrez, and Rebecca Foust, literary family members who have encouraged my writing in general and this work in particular; and Robin Stratton, the kind, patient, wise, beloved head of the literary family that is Big Table Publishing.

Some of these stories have appeared in magazines:

"The Deke" – *Switchback*
"Donuts" – *riverbabble*
"Dough Boy" – *Sugar Mule* and *SFWP Journal*
"Emerald Beauties" – *SFWP Journal* and *Footnote: A Literary Journal**
"Fig Tree Gazing" – *Compass Rose* and *SFWP Journal*
"Iris Descending" – *Weave*
"Kool Brother Rat" – *Write Side Up*
"A Man Forbid" – *94 Creations* and *SFWP Journal*
"Night Bloomer" – *Doorknobs & Bodypaint*
"One Good Thing" – *The Writers Post Journal*
"Our World, Your Home" – *Two Words For Fiction*
"The Petting Zoo" – *Many Mountains Moving*
"Rear View" – *riverbabble*
"Woodsmen" – *riverbabble*
"Worms" – *Prick Of The Spindle*

*"Emerald Beauties" was a Shortlisted Finalist and a Notable Mention for Alternating Current's 2016 Charter Oak Award for Best Historical Fiction.

"But just the same, all I kept saying to everybody was, 'I want to go home.'"
~ Dorothy, *The Wizard Of Oz*

Table of Contents

Tree House

The problem was, Darren wanted a tree house.

He wanted a tree house, and he wouldn't let go.

"But we'd have to... mess up that beautiful tree!" said Kenneth in a thin, reedy voice, with the grin that had reassured his son through eleven years of life: I'm your dad, I love you, and I want what's best for you.

But Darren perceived something strained in the grin, and cocked his head as the new pup did when you chattered at him like an excited chimp.

"Don't you remember, pal? We bought this house so you could climb that great tree! Remember what you said at the open house? You said, I'm gonna climb that tree and see the Pacific—like Núñez de Balboa!" Kenneth shook his head in proud disbelief at his son's precocious store of knowledge. "Núñez de Balboa. Or Columbus sighting the Bahamian shore! Or a pirate in the crow's nest, looking out for the Royal Navy." Kenneth wound a pale, doughy arm around Darren's neck in a piratical way. "Dare," he counseled, "you couldn't climb high enough to do any of those things if we buil—" he choked back the word *built*— "if we put a tree house down there where those limbs fork at the... the..."

"Crotch," Darren sighed, frowning at the grass and grinding his toe into it. The pup nipped his foot and his smile sprang back, and he chased Magellan into the massive hydrangea bushes with their pink and blue blooms that thrived in the deep shade beneath the oak tree. It was a marvelous oak, twenty-five-feet high with a twenty-foot spread, and limbs enough for a multi-tiered village of tree houses.

"Hey, Dare," hollered Kenneth, "this grass is kind of high, doncha think? I'd better push that new mower over it, kinda show it who's boss, you know?" Kenneth strode purposefully into the suburban garage, which was half as large as the apartment they'd left behind in San Francisco, hoisted the mower with difficulty and supported it against the cushion of belly that strained against his *Mind Matters* tee, eschewing the easy course of rolling the mower into the yard so that he could show off his strength. But the wheel banged into the door frame, and Kenneth stumbled awkwardly into the yard as the mower thudded onto the grass. "No harm," he grinned, "missed my toes completely! Guess I'd better wear work boots, huh, son?" He looked down at Darren with paternal gravity. "There's a lesson for you, Dare—don't work in flip-flops! A guy got his toe messed up big time once when a hammer dropped on his foot when he was wearing flip-flops." Kenneth marveled at the prostrate mower as if at a felled tiger. "Man," he said. "That sucker must weigh thirty pounds at least."

To Dad, Darren was Borg Boy. When new information was available for acquisition, he would rotate his head, widen eyes that his father called "information-admitting apertures," and download the data to his "blood-engorged hard drive" for processing and storage. Having processed the content of his father's cautionary advice—and having registered as well its awkward delivery for future decoding—he flopped onto the grass to wrestle the pup as his dad clomped upstairs to put sneakers on.

Kenneth blamed himself. A writer at an educational software firm who understood visual learning, he had shared *Stand By Me* with Darren the night before to show him what boys were like in the Fifties, when Grandpa Jack was a boy. Sitting cross-legged on the living room floor during this inaugural Friday Night At The Movies—"our new tradition," Kenneth had gleefully announced while passing out candy—Darren's aperture-eyes and O-ring mouth had gaped at boys in white tees and cuffed jeans playing chicken with trains, camping out in the woods, firing a gun for the hell of it, running for their lives from a junkyard dog, and, best of all somehow, playing cards and smoking and hanging out in a tree house. "Grandpa was the coolest kid ever!" Darren had said at the end of the film. "Totally the awesomest man in the world!" He had perceived undefined pain in his dad's jagged smile, but he saw no point in dwelling on matters he did not understand, and had immediately rushed to the computer to research tree houses.

He continued his research as Kenneth strained against the push mower, and returned to the yard brimming with excitement.

"Oh hey, Dare, I showed that sucker who's boss," said Kenneth, standing in the center of the lawn with his hand resting on the handle of the mower. Darren mirrored his father's proud smile, and Kenneth tossed two handfuls of grass up over their heads like confetti.

"I found some plans for a tree house," said Darren with a smile that rose high but pulled his father's down low.

"That's great, Dare. But it's not just a question of building it, you know. Safety's the main thing, where my best friend's concerned. I mean, do we even know if the tree can support all that weight? Do we even know if its roots are alright? Or if the tree house won't blow down in the wind? As you know, Dare, when the wind blows, the cradle will rock!"

With the cool objectivity of an actuary, Darren said: "Grandpa can sell you insurance for that."

"He wouldn't sell us insurance, first off, Dare. And second, I don't care about money, I care about your life and limb. And speaking of limbs, how do we even know if the branches are thick enough to support a tree house?"

Darren had no answer, so he charged back inside to sit down at the Mac with tortilla chips and a glass of Country Time lemonade that his mom called *homemade* with an ironic grin.

"Since when do we eat at the computer?" Kenneth asked Pam, who had nestled into the giant cloth-covered cushions of the beige couch.

"Since when do you care?" said Pam, flipping a card into an overturned top hat from last weekend's housewarming hot toddy party.

"The boy spends too much time on the computer," Kenneth declared with the air of an old-fashioned patriarch. Pam raised a brow at her technophile hubby, who added, "I mean, too much time when it's nice out like this. And school ends in two weeks. So if he's gonna be on the computer, it should just be for homework." Pam mewled like a randy cat at Kenneth's uncharacteristic forcefulness, and Kenneth puffed his big body up: "Darren," he said. "You need to go out. We didn't spend our last dime on a house with a yard so you could be a couch potato on a gorgeous Saturday, son."

Darren appealed to his mom with a look, but Pam's commitment to relaxing on weekends encompassed parenting duties, so she just gave him a cool little smile and flipped another card at the hat. Darren knit thick brows that belonged to neither parent and poured his lemonade down the drain in protest of their tyranny, then marched out into the yard and sat cross-legged beneath the oak tree, fuming. When his anger cooled he gazed up at the limbs like a structural engineer surveying a challenge.

Kenneth plopped down next to Pam. "Tree house," he said with a confidential grin implying that the word, the concept, or both, were absurd. The pair twined their fingers and gazed at the home they'd worked for ten years to buy—he for four years as an internet writer and six at the educational-software firm, she as a chat-room moderator and then a community-college counselor. It was not an especially large home, but it seemed large with its open floor plan and high ceiling, and the mellow blond wood that glowed in the light that filtered through the double glass door and wraparound windows.

Darren marched to the Mac like a man on a mission.

"I told you to spend time in the fresh air, Dare."

"You told me to do my homework on Saturday," said Darren, secure in the rectitude of his position. He set himself down at the pinewood dining table in sight of his parents and lowered his head, and kept it lowered as he burrowed through his homework. Pam nuked mac-and-cheese and frozen apple pie for dinner, and they watched a cooking show as they ate. It was dark when they finished, so Darren knew he would not be kicked outside when he seated himself before the computer to research tree houses further.

"Eight inches, dad!"

Pam raised an amused brow at Kenneth, who loaded up a jowl-shaking, "What?"

"Eight inches," repeated Darren with a peevish tone that surprised his folks and himself. "The branches need to be at least eight inches thick to support a tree house at four attachment points. We can measure it tomorrow, or we can go out now if we have a—"

"Darren!" said Kenneth, "I'm not going out *now*." He wrapped his arm around Pam's shoulders, and she, surprised, set her crossword down and snuggled up against hubby's warm, soft flank. "It's Parent Time, Dare."

"I thought Parent Time was on—"

"*And* we're watching *Nat Geo*. It's about Roman engineering, buddy—the amazing aqueducts, this special waterproof concrete they developed for their bridges." He patted the sofa. "You should see it, tiger. You'll get some awesome ideas for those bridges you're building in *Ancient Wonders II*."

"No," sniffed Darren, "it's Parent Time," and marched from the room.

The next day, a Sunday, Mr. Dan, the Vietnamese gardener, stood in the center of the mown lawn facing Kenneth. He was a wiry man with a narrow granite face carved into canyons by the broad smile that was his main means of communicating with customers. Three feet behind him stood his wife in her pyramidal rice-paddy hat, gazing pleasantly at the two men. Kenneth gestured at the knot-holed fence that he wished to replace, and Mr. Dan's smile affirmed that the job could be done, and at a good price.

Pam emerged from the sofa and beckoned Kenneth to the sliding-glass-door.

Ask him to put in some flowers, she said.

What kind?

Nice ones, she said, and sipped her mimosa.

The fence and the flower-bed questions settled, Kenneth stepped over to the oak tree and pointed up at its limbs, then signed a square, meaning *tree house*. Mr. Dan fingered his stubbly chin as he studied the tree through narrowed eyes, calculating, Kenneth supposed, all manner of technical and logistical questions. Uncomfortable with the suspense, Kenneth looked furtively around and noticed Darren watching him through the sliding-glass-door. His face reddening, he grabbed Mr. Dan's arm and pointed emphatically at the tree's upper branches and mimed pruning. Darren sighed, trudged over to his mom, flopped face-down onto the sofa.

It was a Wood Man tradition, the first weekend of summer, for the three generations of Wood males to drive up to Humboldt to visit Great Grandma. Darren had something special on his laptop for her, his final school project, a report about an inspiring family member. He had originally intended to use his dad, but had cooled to the idea over the tree house issue. Then he had considered Grandpa Jack, whom he revered, but had rejected that idea when Grandpa deflected his request for help building a tree house on vague but important-sounding grounds that Darren lacked the adult ken to refute, but suspected of being a pretext. So he choose Great Grandpa Eldon, whom he really considered the ultimate awesomest Wood anyway, except that he was dead. "And really," he told Kenneth and Grandpa Jack as they rolled through the coast redwoods which, to Darren, personified Great Grandpa, "Great wasn't just awesome, he was superhuman, right? I mean he had to be, to defeat the Eebermensh." *Eebermensch*, Grandpa's winking name for the Germans.

"He was the stuff of legends," affirmed Grandpa with his usual twisted inflection, which distorted the meaning of words the way the funhouse mirrors at the Santa Cruz Boardwalk distorted Darren's body.

There was a shrine to Great Grandpa in the house in Eureka, where Eldon had risen from lumberjack to vice-president of sales for L&M Lumber a mere ten years after World War II ended. Gran G now lived alone in the house, laboriously knitting sweaters for the grandkids with arthritic fingers and arranging wildflowers that she plucked from the redwood flower boxes that covered the railing of the wraparound porch.

Darren burst through the paneled oaken front door hollering "Pie!" Gran G, as always, had timed the pie to his arrival, and he had smelled its aroma upon leaping through the car's open window. He pressed his cheek to Gran G's aproned waist and ran to Great's shrine, known in his lifetime as The Den, to gaze at the model train set that filled the room. Great had built the set with his son's help when Grandpa Jack was ages nine through fourteen, and had developed it further for many more years after Jack tired of standing dumbly by while Great, oblivious to his presence, worked out the set's increasingly sophisticated electronics scheme. Gran G had switched the set on just before Darren's arrival, and the black locomotive pulled the red, yellow, and brown boxcars and the fully laden L&M log car, Darren's favorite, through the snow shed, over the great suspension bridge that spanned the glistening river, past the frozen lake on which tiny people really skated, and through the woodland trees flocked with snow to the L&M lumber mill and yard, where an actual working crane designed by Great stood poised to load a flatcar with logs—and oh, how Darren loved manipulating the levers that lifted the logs onto those cars! No less did he love the working headlights of the engine, the amber glow of the streetlights, the real steam that emerged from the engine's smokestack, the wood smoke billowing from the chimneys of the two-story houses at the edge of town, or the orange firelight glowing behind the paned windows of those houses, which resembled the Greats' own house—which, like the toy houses, always had a wood fire burning.

"You were the luckiest kid in the world, Grandpa!"

Grandpa gazed at the train set with a soft little smile: half carefree kid, half careworn oldster.

"Dad," said Darren, "how come you never had a train set?"

Kenneth deferred to his dad with a look, and Grandpa mumbled something semi-intelligible about feeding the family and the pressures of business, omitting to mention his nightly after-dinner stock-trading marathons in the home-office wine-closet situated behind his bedroom, off-limits to Kenneth.

Kenneth sensed his father's discomfort and changed the subject. "Did you ever notice Great's army uniform, Dare?" He tried to hoist his son by the armpits but couldn't raise him above his shoulders. "Jesus, Dare, you're getting big!" He set the boy down and steered him by the shoulders to a wall on which Great's army uniform hung. Darren pressed his cheek to the drab green wool of the jacket-sleeve and breathed-in the masculine aroma of heroism. A black-and-white photo mounted next to the uniform showed Great at sixteen, awash in bright sunlight, bare-chested, rock-ribbed, hoisting a pickaxe to uproot brush for the CCC. Another showed him a little older, bigger and stronger, raising a hammer while helping to build a logging museum for the WPA. "See why you've gotta learn your alphabet?" quipped Grandpa, hoisting Darren up into his arms and straining to raise him to the level of the pictures.

Said Kenneth: "The kid resembles Great, doncha think?"

Grandpa winced, for he believed his grandson looked like him; but he could not deny the obvious resemblance in the two males' angular bodies, long faces, strong jaw lines and bright eyes.

Darren sensed his grandfather's discomfort. "Grandpa," he said, "what was D-Day?"

"Darren Day," grinned Grandpa, and Darren smiled wryly at the non-answer, a deferential trick he had learned from his father.

"What war was Great in, Grandpa?"

"World War Two," replied Grandpa. "The one after the one that had doughboys." The reference to dough made Darren cry "Pie!" so Grandpa lowered him with shaky arms and the boy shot off to the berry-pie kitchen.

Two days later Grandpa drove home, with Kenneth riding shotgun as always. "*Greatest Generation*," Grandpa grumbled. "Great segregation, great McCarthy Era, great insipid culture, great Vietnam War and great Nixon." Kenneth smiled with the pleasure of being his dad's confidant, but his dad's gaze extended miles down the road.

"Doughboys were soldiers!" Darren said from the backseat, and Kenneth beamed to realize that Darren had just gleaned the fact from a World War I learning game that Kenneth had scripted, and which Darren was playing on his laptop.

"Grandpa," said Darren, "were you in the army?"

"National Guard," said Jack tersely.

"Grandpa guarded the nation," explained Kenneth.

"Did you guard the Eebermensh, Grandpa?"

"I guarded the Constitution," he said, "in America."

"He kept the streets safe," explained Kenneth.

"Like drivers, with insurance?" said Darren, who possessed only a sketchy understanding of Grandpa's business.

"Sure," Granpa said.

"Is it fun, keeping people safe?"

"Sure," Grandpa said. "Though I'd rather make wine."

"Granpa's so good at keeping people safe he can afford to buy lots of wine," said Kenneth.

"Why is the wine so good in Sonoma?" asked Darren. "Is the tare wah better than Napa's?"

"Jesus," Grandpa said with a look at Kenneth, "a chip off the old block. Darrey, let me drive, will you?" But a pop and a flapping came from the rear axle as Jack returned his eyes to the road. The rear end swung hard right like a big fish thrashing so as not to be caught, and Jack jerked the wheel right to reverse the skid. The car straightened, and Jack kept a firm grip on the wheel as the car rolled along on three-and-a-half tires. Jack knew they'd be in danger if the flat wore down to the rim before he could pull over, and fixed his eyes on the cars approaching on the other side of the two-lane road while applying light pressure to the brake pedal to slow the car in a controlled manner. As he stared at an approaching pickup, tapping the break while steadying the wheel, he was conscious that his son and grandson were pulling for him in anxious silence. The tire flapped as Jack edged the car to a grassy shoulder, and shuddered as the rim chunked as the car settled into place off the road.

"Nice job, Dad," said Kenneth with blue eyes atwinkle.

"Still got it," grinned Jack with a floppy mouth. He held up a sixty-two-year-old hand whose skin had begun to loosen like Gran G's and had a few brown spots like hers. "Still steady," he said.

Kenneth smiled with pride, as if he himself had delivered them from danger.

"Are you gonna call the auto club, Grandpa? Dad's a member."

"I don't think that'll be necessary," said Jack with a self-satisfied grin.

The trunk of Jack's car was nothing like Kenneth's. Kenneth's was a toy chest: Frisbees, dog toys, beach towels, CDs, folding chairs, picnic basket, water guns, Nerf toys—everything in a riotous jumble. Jack's trunk was pristine but for four lidded boxes: a large clear plastic box filled with car tools, a second filled with emergency gear, a sturdy black toolbox that he had taken to Kenneth's new house to upgrade the light fixtures in Darren's room, and a well cushioned box that he stocked with wines when he traveled. "Set these back about thirty feet, will you, Kenneth?"

Kenneth took a set of red-and-orange reflective triangles from his father's hands and set them carefully on the traffic side of the shoulder while Jack removed the tire-iron from the trunk. He grinned at his grandson, "Hold this for me, Darren," and the kid's eyes widened like a squire entrusted with the sword of a knight. Jack lifted the flap that covered the spare-tire compartment and unscrewed the handle that secured the spare, then removed his suede coat with contempt for the chilly late-afternoon breeze. With a great inhalation he lifted the spare out of its well, then rotated like a discus thrower and set the tire flat on the ground.

Kenneth stood behind his son with his hands clasped before his crotch like a fig leaf.

"Kenneth, why don't you—" Jack's voice trailed off as he searched for a useful task for his son. "Why don't you set these chocks behind the tires. Then call Mom and tell her I'm late."

Jack stepped to the right side of the car with the jack, but hesitated as if fearful of pain.

Which Darren perceived. "Dad can do that for you, Grandpa."

Jack smiled. "No, Dare. You see, this thing is called jack—like me. It's my job this time."

Jack lowered himself stiffly to his knees, lowered his head like the marble-shooting wizard he had been in the early Sixties, aligned the jack with the jacking point, inserted the turning rod and began to rotate it. His son and his grandson looked silently on. "Help me, Dare," he winked. The boy set his hand on the turning rod, and with his grandfather's warm, soft hand clasping his own, he turned the rod—and beheld the wonder of the car levitating. "Now let's get that tire off of this thing," Grandpa smiled, kneeling by the rear tire and pointing at the wheel. "First we've got to get that hubcap off. Give me the sacred tire-iron, Darrey." Darren reverently handed the tire-iron to his grandpa and watched as Jack inserted the blade between the edge of the wheel-cover and the tire and pried. He repeated the process in several spots and pried off the wheel cover with a grunt. "Now comes the fun part, Darren. Nuts!"

"What's wrong?" asked Darren.

"Nothing," grinned Jack, pointing at the lug nuts.

"Grandpa's making a joke," noted Kenneth. His son registered the fact and waited for an explanation. Perceiving that none would come, he turned to soak up his grandfather's grin.

Jack rested one knee on a clean rag to keep his slacks clean and seated the tire-iron over a nut at an angle parallel to the ground to allow himself to transmit the weight of his body down to the nut along stiffened arms. The nut gave way quickly, and Darren's face brightened as it had at age five when his dad first puffed a dandelion ball into the air at the park. He turned to share the joy with his father, but Kenneth wore a defeated grin; his gaze, vaguely oriented towards the tire, was distant and diffused. "Hold this," Jack said, pressing the lug nut into Darren's hand. Darren measured the nut's heft in his palm, deriving pleasure from its hardness and strength. "Don't lose it, my boy." Jack seated the head of the iron over a second nut, raised himself to a crouch and leaned down on his arms, his triceps rising as if pulled by cables. Even at his age he was lean, as Great had been throughout his long life, and as Darren was now. Darren felt a surge of pride at the hardness of his grandfather's arms, and stole a studious glance at his father's belly—so round, so soft, so nice to jump on when he was little; and his face: so pleasantly round and ruddy and kind. Grandpa pressed the second nut into Darren's hand as a tow-truck rolled past.

"That's Dad's club," said Darren.

"It's a lot of people's club," mumbled Kenneth, and began punching his iPhone after aiming a grave farmer's squint at the black-tinged clouds rolling in from seaward. "Wanna search for the weather report, Dare? Red sky at night, sailor's delight." The sky was not red but gray, but Kenneth never missed a chance to quote Darren's favorite line from *Navigation!*, an exploration game that Kenneth had scripted. But Darren didn't hear, he was pressing down on the tire-iron with Grandpa, the two resembling the marines in the Iwo Jima flag-raising photo. "That's three!" cried Darren as the recalcitrant nut gave way before a great effort from Darren and Jack. The fourth and fifth nuts followed quickly, and Darren fondled the lug nuts he had collected in the deep pocket of his cargo shorts, imagining them ball bearings from a Sherman tank.

Jack seated the iron on the sixth and last nut for an upward pull. The two gave it a try, but it didn't yield. "Better let me go solo on this one, Dare." Darren stepped back as Jack strained against the iron, grimacing with discomfort as steel rubbed against skin that was rarely toughened by manual labor these days except for routine household repairs. "Time to show this sucker who's boss," he told Darren with a reassuring grin. He squatted on his haunches like a weightlifter doing the clean-and-jerk and thrust violently upward, but the iron kicked free and slammed into his mouth with his fists, knocking him backwards and down onto his back.

Jack cursed as he lay on his back like an overturned turtle, but it was a gurgling curse muffled by the blood that pooled in his mouth, for he'd split his lip badly. Kenneth reached his hand down, but Jack knocked it away and rolled stiffly onto hands and knees. It occurred to him that he was in the horsey position, and he turned to Darren with the inviting smile that had cued Darren to mount him when Darren was small; but the smile stretched the gash, and blood thick as syrup poured from his mouth.

"Get me the *mmph*," Jack told Kenneth, pressing the back of his hand to his mouth.

Kenneth fumbled through the emergency box for the first-aid kit and removed a roll of gauze wrapped in plastic. He recalled the Halloween party at fourteen when he'd borrowed his dad's Boy Scout uniform in a pinch, and how he'd joked about its hokeyness while secretly admiring the sash's bright array of merit badges: orienteering, lifesaving, first-aid and more. He remembered how he'd secretly envied his dad the scouting experience, even though none of his big-city friends was a Scout, and even though his dad had quit scouting at sixteen during the Vietnam War era for hatred of the Boy Scout uniform and uniforms in general. Kenneth felt the heat of his father's appraising eyes as he tried to figure out how to open the plastic pouch. At last he noticed that the edges of the pouch were slightly separated where they met at the top, and he fumbled at the separation with stubby fingers. Noticing his dad's frustration, Darren said gently, "I can do it Dad, it's like string cheese," and reached for the roll—but Kenneth knocked the boy's hand away and mumbled "Sorry, Dare." He continued to paw at the roll, and finally managed to pinch both ends and peel the thing open. "Clean your hands," said Jack in a blood-muffled way, so Kenneth cleaned his hands with antiseptic gel and unrolled a length of gauze. He neatly folded the gauze into a compress that he presented to his father like a ring-bearer.

Jack pressed the compress tight to his mouth.

"Do you need a—"

"No," said Jack.

Still the tire needed changing. Kenneth looked askance at the fallen tire-iron, then looked at his dad, who looked at him skeptically, and then at his son, who looked up at him with hope and sympathy.

He bent for the tire-iron. Jack noticed that Kenneth was wearing flip-flops, and noticed Kenneth's misshapen middle toe, too. "Kenny," rasped Jack. "Mind your toes."

Kenny had been Dad's little helper at eight when Jack roofed the tool shed. Jack stood atop a stepladder setting shingles in place while Kenny looked up at him with tools and roofing nails at the ready. Jack asked for the hammer and Kenny reached it up to him; but Kenny released the hammer before his dad's grip was sure, and the hammer fell like a baton in a relay race, its heavy head landing on Kenny's middle toe. The boy's shrill howls, certain to bring his mother tearing into the yard in a panic, elicited a chastising "klutz" from Jack even as he hopped off the ladder to set the boy on his lap and examine the injury. He capably set the bent toe in a splint, but it was a Sunday, and they didn't get Kenneth to a doctor until the next day, when the doctor said there was nothing to do. "It looks like a caterpillar bunching up to crawl along a leaf," Jack said then. His wife repeated the line, and Kenny grinned along with them.

Kenneth set the iron on the recalcitrant nut and squatted low on his haunches like a sumo wrestler, finding it hard to keep his balance. He knew that he had the advantage of bulk, and he looked like a weightlifter as he strained against the iron with a two-handed upward motion, conscious that his son and father were studying him, determined not to lose his grip on the rod with his "two hands full of thumbs," as his dad had once called them.

But the nut didn't budge, and perspiration from exertion and nerves beaded on his brow.

"Dad," said Kenneth, "do we have any—you know, lubrication stuff?"

Jack nodded at the toolbox in the trunk. There was a small canister of WD-40, but the detachable nozzle was tiny, and Kenneth struggled to fit it into the tiny aperture in the canister's head. Darren said, "Let me try Dad, I've got little fingers," and this time Kenneth accepted the help. Darren stuck his tongue out in concentration like the adept model-plane builder Jack had taught him to be, and fitted the nozzle neatly into place. Kenneth cuffed his son's head and sprayed lubricant on the lug nut.

But the nut didn't budge.

"Kenny," said Jack. "We'd better call the auto club."

But Kenneth ignored his father and bent back to his work, jerking at the iron with raw red hands.

"Kenny," said Jack. "I'm calling the club."

Sweat poured from Kenneth's forehead. His haunches trembled. He straightened stiffly and stretched out his shoulders. The westerly breeze chilled the sweat on his brow—it felt good, like swimming in the ocean. He looked down at his son, who had not budged, but gazed at him with hope and belief, like a sports-fan pulling for his favorite player. "You wanna be king, little bud? Pull Excalibur out of the stone."

Darren smiled. "I can't get it out, Dad."

Kenneth bent to his task and thrust upward with a mighty effort.

The nut didn't budge.

"Dare," he said, "get me Grandpa's work-gloves from the toolbox." He put on the oversized canvas gloves and flexed his fists. He looked, he believed, like a falconer.

"Kenny," said Jack. "The truck'll be here soon, buddy."

But Kenneth set his jaw and pulled against the iron with a weightlifter's grimace. The muscles in his hands, arms, and shoulders strained. They would hurt tomorrow: he knew that much, though he had never played sports or lifted weights. And he knew they'd be stronger.

"Dad," said Darren. "What can I do?"

"Nothing," said Kenneth, straining against the iron. His breath was short. "Ten inches," he panted. "The branches need to be ten inches in diameter at the attachment points."

The yellow tow-truck pulled onto the shoulder twenty feet ahead. The driver had a shaved bowling-ball head and a linebacker's build—Kenneth's build, if he lost thirty pounds.

"Darren," he said, straining against the iron as the tow-truck guy made notes on a paper on a clipboard. Sweat glazed Kenneth's vision, but it seemed that the guy grinned derisively at him. "Look up the plans on your laptop, dude. There's a lumber yard on the way home from Grandpa's."

He strained against the iron as the tow-truck guy advanced.

The Deke

Monday: Lunch with the Squirrels

Don't even talk about your dad, Squirrel—my dad's so uncool he puts your dad to shame. D'you know what he does for a living, dude? He sells real estate, dude, do you know what that is? It's *houses*, dawg, he sells houses to rich people, and gets a big, fat commission for basically *nothing*. And if that's not bad enough, he works with landlords who evict people—man, that's so messed up I don't care how liberal his so-called politics are! Now take Deke—*Deke*, that righteous old dude from the open mike! There's a cat who's cool, dawg! Yeah, dawg, I know I said *cat*, that's what they called 'em back in the day—back when Deke was our age. ... No, dude, my dad wasn't our age, ever. But Deke was, and he was already a poet, too—and not just that, he'd already dropped out of school, ming! Did you know they had a slogan for dropouts then? "Tune in, turn on, and drop out!" See, they understood that dropping out meant reaching a higher mental plane or whatever—they were so far ahead of us it's scary. So far ahead of you, anyway. Me? I'm escaping this mind-swamp in a week. ... You've got it, dude, I've made up my mind: I'm selling my stuff and putting a deposit down on that room in the Haight with the Montana twins—or if that falls through, I'll crash on Deke's couch, he's read my poetry and he thinks I've got chops. ... No way, Squirrel, he's not *just a bookstore dude*, that's messed up two ways! First, it's the coolest bookstore on Haight Street. Second, like I told you: Deke was a Beat, man, one of those old-school poets who rhymed like rappers—in fact, Deke says Beats were the original rappers, even better than rappers, 'cause they rhymed on the fly—and with music, dude, with bongos and flutes! ... Bongos, you know, those little twin lap drums we saw at that drum circle. ... No they didn't *sample*, dude—they made music! Aw, forget it, Squirrel, you are so non-retro I can't even believe it! Hey, Squirrel, here comes your Mini Me! Here Squirrely Squirrely, bring your puffy little cheeks on over an' have some beer nuts! Hey Squirrel Man, leave that brew here if you're goin' to class. Four hours school is enough for any Bean.

Tuesday: KFC

You and your popcorn chicken. Thanks to your absurd Squirrely urges, we're stuck drinkin' Pepsi instead of The King! ... What do you mean, *we* can't go to math buzzed? *I'm* dropping out, remember? Besides, since when do you care about tests? ... Yeah, I know how that is—but the difference is, you let your parents squeeze you, and I don't let mine, 'cause I know it only encourages them. It's like Deke says, structure is for the power elite, not for poets and seers. Do you think Jerry Garcia was into structure? ... Yeah, Deke does look like Jerry— right down to the Santa beard and those mad crinkly eyes! Man, they are so not like my old man's eyes. My old man's eyes drill into you, like: "Hey, did you do your homework yet?" and, "Tell me, exactly, how do you expect to make your way in the world without a high school degree?" And of course the famous, "Hey, did you do your homework yet?" It's like, Deke and I were rappin' at the store yesterday with the Montana twins, and someone's like, hey, Deke, you're like Peter Pan, man, you're the leader of the lost boys or somethin'—and Deke just grins and draws this joint out of nowhere, and we all go in back and get high and write this rap song right on the spot, *The Lost Boyz Rap* we called it, and we're drummin' on books and chairs and everything and taking turns rhyming, all these brilliant rhymes, like—well, I don't remember any of 'em exactly, but they were all brilliant, all this great stuff about Peter Pan, and how they *hook* you in school like this principal, Captain Hook, and how they try to keep you scared at home like the kids in the Peter Pan story. Man it was cool. And Deke says, Yeah, well, I'm cool and all that, but I've got some rules, too. Like Rule Number One: Anyone has pot, everyone smokes. And Rule Number Two: No selling. So I keep my sales stash stuffed in my jeans.

Wednesday: Lunch back of the Dumpster

Weird day yesterday, dude. Here, have a hit. First, Deke was weird. I ride my board all the way down to the store and slide in smooth and I'm all *wassup?* —and he just stares at me like I'm a retard. So I'm like, *he's* having a bad day. So I chill and read zines. Then I go, "Hey, Deke, I was wonderin'—what's your real name, man?" And he gets all beady eyed and goes, "What, Deke's not *real* enough for you? I'm *The Deacon*, man, that's all there is to it." And I'm all *whatever.* Then he kinda slumps over and gives me this sad old-rabbi look and says, "Look, li'l dude, you gotta scram. The Boss Man got his panties in a twist 'cause some yuppie princess came in yesterday with no one at the register, and some, quote, *obnoxious people* loudmouthing in back—yeah, *us*—so I've gotta be a Boy Scout for a while." So I'm all, fine, whatever, and I bounce and call Ronnie. He comes over to my house and starts playing guitar, and I start fooling around with that conga my dad got me. So of course, my dad heads straight for my room with this incredible radar he has for spoiling my fun, and sticks his head in the doorway with his puppy dog look and says, "Can I jam?" And I'm thinkin', that is so lame, you don't *ask* "Can I jam?" you just *do* it. So we're all, yeah, whatever, and Ronnie starts playing this Marley tune, and Dad starts playing the other conga, and he's making totally sure we can see how into it he is, like rolling his eyes and moving his head around like, hey, look at me, I'm jamming with my son! Pathetic. ... Yeah, he was good, but he wasn't *good*-good, not *rasta*-good, just good like you're supposed to be—like a TV commercial. A wasted day, Squirrely.

Thursday: Lunch at the Beach

Dude, there's nothing like celebrating the end of the school week with brews at the beach! ... It's not the end? It is for me! End of the school week, end of the school year, end of the school life! ... *High five?* Dude, you are so middle school I can't believe it! Remember, Squirrel

Man, I'll be waiting for you on the outside. ... Yeah you will! You will be, dude, trust me—freedom's über contagious. Mm, good brew. Man, it was pathetic at the bookstore last night. You should see what The Deke has to go through. The Boss Man put an espresso machine in 'cause he's afraid everyone's gonna go all Starbucks on him, so now it's not good enough that The Deke can recite Beat poetry from heart, and was personally busted in the Free Speech Movement and sang folk songs with Pete Ci-gar and everything, now he's got to make coffee for yuppies, too! Like these two guys in rich-boy suits that come in yesterday and order cappuccino—and while Deke's makin' it, they're on their cell phones talking *buy this! sell that!* and all this stock market garbage. Then one of 'em puts his hand over the phone like he's a very big deal and says in this snotty voice, "Excuse me, Mr. Kerouac, could you put a little less froth in my cappo please?" And the other guy cracks up like it's the funniest thing ever! I mean, just 'cause The Deke wears a beret and works on Haight Street, they think he's a damn Disneyland attraction! I'll bet he woulda popped 'em in the mouth if he wasn't saving up for studio time for his spoken word album. ... And he's nonviolent. And sixty, duh. Hey dude, mañana. I've gotta see those Montana boys about that room, and don't give me that weak-ass "It's not The Haight" shit, you can smell the pot, piss, and pizza when the wind blows, so it's Haight enough for me!

Friday: Lunch in the Schoolyard

Dude, you finally turned your cell phone on! Hey, sorry you had to walk the mean streets alone, but I closed that—ahem—*business* deal this morning, and I'm moving in with The United Dropouts of America, Montana chapter, pronto. ... Hey, I said I'm sorry, dude, you shoulda had your cell phone on! Just lay low in the shadows and the bad boys won't bug you. ... Sure thing, Squirrel, we will definitely get popcorn chicken next week. ... I'll miss you too, man—those long lunches together, cutting class ... Well of course I remember the firecrackers in the can! And dude, who can ever forget cheerleading practice, cha! And the Physics Club! And Debate Club! And those AP classes! And of course, who can ever forget hanging out with the pretty people making snide remarks at the nerds! What? You can? Ha! You should drink some beer, Squirrely. Oh yeah, you've got class, lucky boy ... Mm, that's good. Omigod! I'm drinking alone! One of the top ten warning signs of alcoholism! Well this don't count, it's a special occasion ... erp! Lemme ask you somethin', Squirrely. Did you ever think about the difference between us and our folks? The difference is, they're all noun obsessed, and we're all about verbs. Take dropping out. I'm *dropping out*. It's a verb. It's something I'm *doing. Just* something I'm doing. I'm still Jack The Beanstalk, I still smile like a pumpkin, I still love rhymes, and I still stick up for my friends—always. But to my dad, *dropout* is a noun, and that's what I *am*—or will be in a day. That's why he's all, "Don't be a dropout, Jack!" Like if I drop out, all of a sudden I won't be "Jacko" anymore, or "best pal" or "hoopster." I'll just be: *Dropout*. See, it's all nouns and verbs, it explains everything. You know, I bet I could ace English in a minute if I wanted to ... as if.

Monday: The Last Lunch

This is it, dude, the last supper—one last lunch for The Squirrel and The Bean. ... Heck yeah I'm going through with it! But—the "it's" different now. How? Well, my last day of school was Friday, right? And I celebrated by cutting. Well, guess who decided to notice I was still alive all of a sudden? Dean J. And he called my dad to tell him I cut, and Dad went all over town looking for me, and found me at the bookstore, chillaxing with Deke. And it was like—a showdown, man, like *The Matrix*. First, they're kinda checkin' each other out, like gunfighters. And Dad looks at me and goes, "You're not in school," which was the *duh* of the day—but he can't get too mad, 'cause Deke's there, and Dad's working on his Dad Of The Century medal. And Deke goes, "Maybe I oughta let you and the youngblood work this out in private." So Dad goes all formal on him and says, "Excuse me, we haven't met. I'm Dan Campbell." And he sticks his hand out for a business-type handshake, but Deke gives him a soul shake instead. And then all of a sudden, they start chit chatting like I'm not even there. It was—weird. They were like, kissing up to each other, like some bizarro adult conspiracy or something. Then Deke starts talking about how bad the book business is with the chain stores and the internet taking over, and my dad's all, hey, I hear you. Then Dad goes, hey, I've heard you're quite a poet, Jack's told me all about you— except, it sounds like he's trying to hold in a crap. And Deke goes, "Yeah, The Bean's got a great ear," and Dad looks at me and says "*The Bean*" real low, as if it's totally lame to be called that—as if I haven't told him a million times my friends call me *The Bean*! Then Dad gives The Deke this look and says, "You know, man, I've written some poetry myself." He actually says *man*! "I'd rather be doing what you're doing than selling real estate any day." And I'm puking. Then Deke nods at me and goes, "Well, hey, you know, you really oughta encourage this guy's poetry, he's drying up in that so-called school, that sameness factory." So Dad does a complete 'tude 180. He snaps his head back and says, "Excuse me? You're telling me how to be a father to my boy? *You're* telling *me*?" And Deke goes, "I'm not *telling* you, man, I've just been there—and I've picked up quite a few things on the road." And I'm all, The Deke was a dad? Then I remember The Deke saying he had a kid once, but he split when the kid was still just a kid, and the kid's grown now, and he tracked The Deke down and they had a few beers—I guess I'd suppressed it, repressed it, whatever, 'cause that's not too cool. So my dad's all, "You shelter runaways, and you shelter truants, and you're lecturing me on raising my son?" And Deke's all, "Just listen to yourself, man, labeling him *my son*." It's the noun thing, see? Deke goes, "Sure you begot him, and sure, you've given him your best shot and all—but this *my son* stuff is a power trip, man, he belongs to the universe—like we all do. And sooner rather than later, you gotta give him up to the wonder." And Dad's eyes are popping like ping pong balls, the veins on his forehead are all pumped up like when Mom tells him to lie down for his blood pressure. He's all "*Give him up*? You mean, give up *on* him, don't you? Well I've got news

22

for you, my fine feathered friend, *giving up* is not in the Campbell vocabulary—though it may be in yours." And he keeps on blasting Deke, and it was—cool, sort of. And while Dad's sputtering at him, Deke's giving me this look, like rolling his eyes and smirking at me. And what was really funny was, it was the same look you gave me behind the Princely Pal's back when he ripped into me for board sliding that rail last week. So Dad finishes his rant and he's all, "Let's go, Jack," but I can see from his face he's not sure I'm coming, cuz it's the same look he had when he came to grab me away from that bonfire at the beach last year after curfew, and I didn't go that time. And I'm not sure I'm going this time, either. So he turns to go, and I just sit there. Then all of a sudden, this force kind of pulls me off the stool like a water skier being towed by a boat. And I go with him. ... What? ... No, it's not the last time I ever will. ... I'll tell you what I mean. What I mean is, I've had it with his bullshit and Mom's bullshit, and how they always know best, because their life's so great, always, "Oh, the bills" and, "Oh, the stress" and, "Oh, my blood pressure," oh yeah, they know best, like tossing a few bucks to the food bank and catching a play now and then make them all that, and they own me and my life, 'cuz I'm just a fool who doesn't know jack.

So you know how he's always threatened to put me in The Phoenix, that last-chance school for misfits? Well, he put the fix in with Dean J to get me transferred there—and I'll tell you, the dean and the Princely Pal couldn't be happier, 'cause the school GPA is gonna go up about a point with me gone! So Dad gets his TV voice on and says, "This'll straighten you out, Jack. They won't tolerate any of your nonsense, and they'll challenge you, too. And believe me, son—you're gonna come out of it a stronger person." Oh, I believe you, Dad, father always knows best—except when he doesn't—and he don't. And to prove it, I'm playin' him. ... How? By doing the exact opposite of what he expects. By showing up at the new school every day, and doing every damned thing I'm supposed to do, just so I can look him in the eye the glorious day I leave home for good and say, "See, Dad? I did everything you asked me, and I still hate school, and I'm still not going to college, and I'm still not gonna be a robot like you and Mom, ever." Then he'll see I was right all along, and I'll be done with his bullshit forever. Hey I'll drink to that. Ah-*ah*-ah-ah-*ah*-ah-ah-*ahhhhhhhh-men*!

Worms

Had anyone ever sung this as a blues? "Nobody likes me, everybody hates me, think I'll go eat worms." But he sang it as a teardrop dirge, dripped straight into the freshly-dug earth. It was good soil, rich and thick, black as charcoal, and he gathered a handful and gazed as if it held all the answers.

Maybe worms did. One worm, fat with life, grayish-pink and semi-translucent, waved its protruding flesh in the air as if seeking mooring, or saying hello.

"Don't eat it, Dad!"

To the child he looked like the fly-eating Renfield, but Dad's mouth was only widened in wonder.

"Earthworm's are a*maz*ing, Johnny." He lowered his face to the ground like an abject slave, and delivered his words in a trembling hush. "They aerate the soil and—" his voice broke and crumbled into the hole.

"Are you gonna come eat?" The child knew the question was a gamble, and because he resented having to gamble and was fearful, his tone cloyed. His father shuddered, and the gamble was lost. "Are you gonna plant something new tonight, Dad?"

"The worm's such a beautiful thing, John." The man gazed with reverence at the worm, which, as if grateful for the reverence, spiraled and touched a dirt-caked finger. The dad chuckled in the hysterical fashion of an airline passenger when the plane has stabilized after a twenty-foot drop. The boy stood rooted, facing his father, and inflated his shoulders with a long inhalation. He longed for his dad's gaze, he had missed it for weeks; but he feared it, too, for its desperation and lack of control. He wanted to climb onto his dad's back, which was rounded like a turtle's, and press his face against the black fleece, and hold on tight as his father rose up like a mighty island, and smell his neck, and feel his bristly beard carving tracks of manhood into his cheek. The boy wanted to kick his dad, too, and this checked the impulse to jump on his back.

The kitchen window slid open with an emphatic click. The boy was conscious of his mother silently watching but did not turn around. Then a psychic force like a hammer-blow crumpled him to his knees right next to his father, who smiled with gratitude but withheld his gaze.

"This worm's our friend, John, like all living things. We're all in this together, you know." The father reached for his son's hand, but hesitated as if reaching to pet an unknown dog. Then he remembered himself and cupped his son's hand, and lowered the worm, and the clod that encased, it into the boy's palm. The boy widened his eyes as the worm waved in the air like a snake charmer's cobra, but he understood the new rules, and did not look at his dad. He thought of his mother and ran in for dinner.

Dinner was odd, it had been odd for months. They ate in the nook—not *they*, but the boy, for she didn't eat, but flitted around the kitchen in a facsimile of purposeful action. The boy called her "hummingbird," though her face sagged like dough, and she called herself "slug" and avoided his eyes as his father did now. "You're always moving around like a hummingbird," he insisted, and she banked with spread wings and swooped in to kiss the top of his head, but still didn't smile. "You need to eat," the boy told her. "Sit," he added with forcefulness that startled them both.

She checked the pedometer. "What, are you kidding?" and busied herself with the coleus and cacti in the window. When she thought her son wasn't looking, she looked out into the vegetable garden that had been a weed jungle just three months before and narrowed her eyes at her husband kneeling in the dirt with his arms upraised like a praying mantis.

"You need to eat," repeated the boy, sensing that he alone understood the proper order of things.

"What, *that?*" she exclaimed with a dismissive wave.

He looked at his spaghetti. It looked good enough. "They're worms!" he said brightly. "They're good for the soil." She sagged onto her arms on the counter. He sensed weakness in her resistance. "Worms are our friends, Mom. Dad's friends with all things."

"Oh, is he?" The boy knew from his mother's tone that she wouldn't sit down on the bench next to him to snuggle up close. Her body had changed, she was wasting away: thirty-five pounds of motherly comfort lost since mid-winter, and it was only just spring.

The boy's father, once paunchy, had lost weight too, for he would not eat, unlike the boy's mother, who could not. The dad had grown hard when the garden project sheared fat from his frame like clay from a sculpture to reveal a lank, long-limbed figure unlike that which had reposed with his wife through long TV evenings of buttered popcorn and soft neutral words. Then came The Thing, and then his confession, the sides of her fists pounding his chest as if to crack ribs, the thought sizzling in her mind that a shard of bone might impale his heart. He had stood shame-faced until she was spent, and remained motionless as she sucked their marriage deep within herself.

No praying man he, but he made every promise he could imagine—to his wife, to himself, to the gods he didn't believe in, to the weeds. The first promise was to establish the garden. It was not a promise he expressed verbally to her, for he could not speak and she would not listen, but a vow to the essence of goodness in the ether to provide life-giving gifts for the sake of his family: tomatoes rich red and shining with life, kale deep green with rubbery ribs for massaging intestinal walls, broccoli that would turn bright green with steaming, carrots so sweet that Johnny's school lunches would be the coolest in class, and radish bunches for Johnny to twine in soil-encrusted fingers—all to be harvested day after day in a huge woven basket, she loved woven baskets, they had a picture book of Pomo Indian baskets, and after The Thing he had driven two hours in a rainstorm to buy this basket for her. She'd shoved it beneath the kitchen table and it rested there still, and he sanctified it by letting it be.

The hardscape had taken a full nine weeks. He knew this because he had logged his work in a journal in which he accounted for every cent spent on the project and maintained his planting plan for the garden's first season. The hardscape was a triumph for one who had rarely worked with his hands, a three-foot-wide roughhewn brick path leading from the kitchen to a three-tiered, ten-foot-wide brick planter. Working with brick meant constantly blooding the earth with his knuckles, and this yielded nervous satisfaction. When the last brick was laid he did not savor the triumph, but stood back like an artist and asked aloud, as if seeking guidance: "What now?"

The answer: more work. Every spare minute after work, and all day on weekends, he dug three-foot-deep holes for the fruit trees to be planted adjacent to the planter, though two would suffice, hoisted hernia bags of organic planting mix for the fruit trees and the planter, enriched the mix with kitchen-scrap compost, a crumbly black miracle, and inhaled deeply the heady aroma of residual earth packed beneath his nails.

Now it was planting time, and he lifted herb seedlings from their little cell packs with the nervous wonder of a father holding his babe in the delivery room, and patted them into place in their moist pouches of earth with the care of a father strapping a baby into a car seat. He sifted the fairy dust at the crown of the root balls, then pressed the backfill into place as tenderly as he would tuck his son's blanket after the boy's mother left the room. It grew dark, and he worked by lantern-light in pious observance of their nightly ritual. The kitchen window clicked shut, and he turned to see the light disappear; this meant it was safe to go in, for she scrupulously honored their unspoken bargain. This night he had a surprise for her, a spry basil seedling of Peter Pan-green that he patted into place in a small terra cotta pot meant for her garden array on the kitchen-window sill. Perhaps this would nudge her to cook as she should, as he did, with fresh herbs and olive oil, not butter and salt, for the sake of their health and a long, happy life together. He set the seedling upon the sill. In the bright down-light of the sill in the otherwise-dark kitchen, the young plant looked like a nightclub singer taking a solo.

The click of the phone as he trudged up the stairs, a click with the softness he considered her essence: soft gaze, soft voice, soft womanly curves awaiting his touch in their four-poster bed with its white canopy and white comforter, the bedroom a shrine to conjugal bless. But he'd slept on the floor the first night of The Thing, 'til she jabbed him awake with a toe to the ribs and a choking, seething, "Get up." They slept now not touching, their backs to each other.

"How's Corey," he said with false nonchalance.

"Fine," she said warily.

"How's his friend," he said, alluding to the rumor that Corey was gay, and thus no threat to him.

"He's fine, too." Her eyes glittered with guilty satisfaction at his insecurity, for Corey was not gay in fact, and cared for her deeply.

He tromped to the bathroom, and returned to darkness.

Johnny stuck his tongue out as he drew with a black crayon clutched in his fist like a dagger.

"What's that?" asked his mom, mildly disturbed by the serpentine figure spanning the paper.

"It's a worm eating glass. Worms eat glass, Dad says."

The woman raised her eyebrows, poured fresh-squeezed orange juice—the man insisted on fresh—and detested herself for caring that he'd be pleased if he passed through the kitchen. "What's that?" She pointed at the baseball cap atop the worm's head and the long black curls cascading from beneath it.

It was the father's cap and his newly long hair. The mother knew that, and the boy knew that she knew, and ignored her. Then he made the red crayon pour blood from his dad's mouth due to the glass in his wormy gullet. The woman rolled her eyes up like a murder victim, then rolled them over to the new plant on the window sill, as tender as her son and as needful of care. Her husband was out in the morning chill, on the ground on his knees like a child at play, placing plastic sheeting over the bed of strawberry seedlings. She imagined the succulence of slices of sun-warmed strawberries scattered over pound cake and drenched in fresh cream, then blanched at the thought of the cake and the cream. What was she like, The Other Woman? Thin, no doubt.

Worse—maybe not. Her hand shot upward, but an act of will stayed it from strangling the basil seedling that mocked her Midwestern dowry of savory casseroles as creamy and comforting as her mother's warm kitchen. Who was this man to deny her her *self*, with his sanctimonious zeal for fresh food, its healthfulness and color, with messianic eyes implying the right food could save the world—it's what he had always wanted, to save the world, the sweet loving world, including her—and she'd loved him for that. But this wasn't that, it was just a cheap trick to make her lose weight. Or maybe it wasn't. Doubt hammered her head and she reached for her pills, then gathered herself back into herself and filled the little brass watering can and sprinkled the coleus and the geranium plant and the row of succulents they'd purchased on their trip to Death Valley—but she bypassed the basil with a twisted grin.

Come Sunday he planted tomato starts in the terraced brick planters with a sanctified air, encasing each in an inverted frame of conical wire. There was a pleasing regularity in the spacing of the structures, like the towering hilltop columns of wind turbines the family would pass on their way to Yosemite. "These are bringing us power," he'd tell his son with a gleam, and Johnny would raise flexed arms and scowl mightily. Now Johnny, wearing a black eye-patch, clambered up onto the third and highest planter four feet above ground and spread his legs like a pirate captain and looked down contemptuously at his kneeling dad. Unlike other neighborhood gardeners who had just emerged from their winter-time hibernation with their radios tuned to spring baseball or public radio, this man worked in silence and never looked up, though he derived comfort from the proximity of his son. "We'll be eating pretty in three months, Johnny Boy," the father said.

"I dub you Sir Sneaks-A-Lot," the boy snarled, pointing his toy sword at his father's neck and awaiting eye contact that never came, for his dad's head fell as if a cable had snapped.

From the kitchen the wife saw the droop of her husband's head and his prostration, and detected a vacuum into which she might speak. The words she wafted quivered like sparrows: "Lemonade, Johnny." She meant her famous fresh-squeezed with a mint sprig in the pitcher. Johnny waved his sword across his domain, glowing with power. "Lemonade," she called, her brittle voice implying that Dad was invited too. Dad's back was to the kitchen and his face to the soil, but he nodded reverently at the infant plants glistening elvin-green in the sunlight, standing tall and proud as children on a formal occasion. The drumbeat of a hammer two houses over snapped him back to work.

When evening approached he rose to go in, but lingered to gaze at the garden, which was saturated in golden fairy light. He noticed the kitchen light on, and removed his sneakers and banged them together loudly, as if dislodging mud, to warn his wife of his approach. The light stayed on, and he entered the house. His wife and son sat in the nook before their plates: for the first time in months, they had waited for him. The woman sat with her head to the plate talking in a hush to her son, her frame of hair glowing honey-brown in the light of an amber bulb. He longed to disappear into her hair, but her face was gaunt, it had lost the roundness that suited her mane: she was a wigged skull in a Day of the Dead shrine. Emotion urged him to leap the table, inflate her with a kiss, restore her to health and himself. "Nice dinner," he murmured.

She nodded as if this were not likely. He slid in beside her and she recoiled on reflex, then collected herself and sat erect. Their son, across the table, stared up at his gods with intense curiosity and growing suspicion. The boy's father looked down into dark little eyes rimmed with blackness, and blinked mirthlessly. "Let's eat," the dad said, and the boy grabbed a dinner roll with both hands and tore in. Father and son appeased angry stomachs with linguini in olive oil with capers and roasted red peppers. "This'll go great with our homegrown toms and basil," the man told his wife as he looked at his son, but when he glanced at the sill, he saw that the basil seedling had withered. With an effort he held back from complaining, but his wife's silence vexed him. He noticed that she hadn't taken a bite, and this vexed him too. "You need to eat," he told her in a tone that had sprung from a well of concern but been polluted by pique on its way out his mouth. She grabbed her son's hand and locked her jaw shut.

When dishwashing time came the man stood with a towel in his hand, and his son squinted up at a giant redwood and the halogen sun over his head. The man looked down benevolently at his son and apprehended wonder and awe, and patted his head with a healing touch. The phone rang on schedule. The woman turned to her husband with fear and vindictiveness frozen in her features, and he gazed back with the warmth he had shone on his son. Within the woman's gaze burned malice and vengeance, bloodletting and guilt. The man's smile slackened to wistful melancholy. The phone pulsed on, each single beat a blow at their tendril-thin bond. The man quivered and hardened. The woman remained still. The phone relented and the two breathed again. Their mood was that of a first-date couple who've gone too far: smoothing rumpled clothes, making awkward jokes with averted eyes, wondering what their coupling means. They didn't know, and neither spoke of it.

The woman took her son upstairs for story time, leaving her husband alone in the kitchen to commune with the window-sill garden beneath the lone light. The dirt in the basil pot was crusty and dry. The man stroked it with a finger, then drew two fingers up the stalk to support the withered lower shoots. The plant was near death: this was his wife's doing: he apprehended his wife in the plant. Beneath the false moonlight he tweezed the caked dirt and pulverized it, filled the little brass watering can with tepid water and a few drops of an iron-zinc solution, sprinkled it onto the dirt and massaged the moistened dirt with his fingers. He caressed a downcast leaf. He jammed a kitchen skewer into the soil and tethered the plant, then polished the watering can while gazing at the plant.

The telephone renewed its assault. The man seized up and counted. At five rings he stopped counting, and marched out into the night to pluck snails.

Dough Boy

At nine years old, he was *Duke* for a day.

"Where are you going, Mikey?" A note of alarm wormed into Mom's voice. Three weeks since moving in, he had not ventured out.

"I'm *Duke* now. Goin'a play." The conk of wooden bats on the asphalt, the sweet siren song of boys in the street.

"*Out?*" Her cookie-dough hands kneaded each other red. She studied her son: his dumpling chin set, his furry brow knit. "Have fun out there. *Duke*," the forced note of cheer for herself more than him. She reached for his ball cap to straighten the bill, was shocked when he jerked his head from her hands.

Thus *Duke* ventured out.

"Duke," sneered the leader, a crewcut called Butch. "You're, like, The Duke of Earl, man?"

Duke chewed Dubble Bubble, stared up through eyes sheltered deep in dark sockets.

"Don't you, like, *talk*, Duke Man?"

"Sure he does." A blond scarecrow called Skeeter clapped Duke on the arm. "He said his name's *Duke*. Like, put up your dukes," and mimed boxing moves.

"Right," Butch grinned, feinting towards Duke like a boxer in close. "You like using your dukes, Dukey boy?"

Duke rooted to the grass, stared up in wonder at Butch.

"Weird little troll, tell you that much."

"You bat first, Duke," said Pee Wee with a not-unkind smile.

Middle of the street, pitch the ball to yourself. Up ball, grab bat, swing bat, miss ball. Again. Again. Then once again with his tongue sticking out and sweat bubbles bursting. Boys' mitts on their heads crowning popping clown faces.

"It's, like, a magic wand," Pee Wee grinned without malice. "Like that guy on *Ed Sullivan* who kept those balls in the air without touching his wand. Like the wand repelled 'em."

They grinned. So did Duke.

"What're *you* smiling at, dick head?"

"Hello, *Duke*." She tried her best to make it sound real.

"I'm *Dick* now." He compressed jagged lips, scrunched his dark brow intently. She laid down the spatula and reached for her boy. He collapsed within himself, and she held back for fear he'd explode.

"I don't think you should play with those boys, Michael."

The tears burst, and he stomped to his room.

She bought him a cowboy hat and a cap gun, a chemistry set, a model T-Bird with a full set of paints, a model World War II battleship. The chemistry set took.

Hour on hour, alone at his desk, he filled beakers precisely and measured out powdered chemicals in tiny spoons to make fizzes, colors, sizzles, stinks. The stink bomb freaked the dog, who ran wildly in circles. The invisible ink was runny but worked. Spy notes to his mother, placed in the dog's collar, ferried to the kitchen. His mom played along and scrawled: *Brownies in ten minutes, hon.* He cut her reply into dozens of little squares, dissolved them in a phosphate solution, hunkered back down to work.

His dad, in the doorway, was hip to it all. "How's it goin', Professor?"

Professor! A jagged grin turned halfway to Dad, and then back to work. He prepared a fuel of baking soda and vinegar that propelled a boat across the bathtub. Buoyed by his success, a new mission was planned: to launch a missile from the front lawn. However, the lawn was an insecure zone with bad boys afoot, so Mission Control postponed the launch. *Captain America, Batman,* and *Mad* indoors. Tag with the dog. Itching powder on the dog's skin, washing her off with hose-water and tears. TV days turned to weeks, and school days to months; then John Glenn flew, and the mission was on. He marched to the front-lawn launching pad on a clear-sky Saturday at morning cartoon time, the rocket thin and red, the launching pad filled with baking soda and vinegar for massive propulsion. The backyard test launches had all been successful. Goggles up; missile in. Three figures on Schwinns soared up the street. He turtled over the launching pad and heard, but did not see, Butch, Skeeter, and Pee Wee whizzing past; he didn't see Pee Wee peeling off like a fighter pilot and wheeling towards him in a wide graceful arc up the slope of his lawn.

"Whatcha doin', man?"

He didn't look up, too intent for distraction. "Missile launch," he said, and added some phony technical mumbles. He prepared to shake up the launching pad, then remembered his dad's admonitions. "You gotta back up," he told Pee Wee. Pee Wee—not *wee* now, just a bit undersized—smiled amiably and backed up his bike. Pleased with his eminence, *The Professor* mumbled a private incantation, shook the launching pad and pointed it at the sky. Fizz-whoosh-whizz and up flew the missile, but not very high. Foamy vinegar flowed down his fist, an acrid smell pinched his nostrils.

"Ai right," Pee Wee smiled, respecting the effort. He stood up on the pedals of his three-speed and piston-charged into the wild blue yonder.

"Is your name *The Professor*?" they giggled.

All girls were from space, but especially these two: pretty and tall, with inscrutable laughter and a cryptic conversational code. Did they wish to hug him and call him their mascot, like big sister Jill's giggly high school friends? Or did they simply think him a jerk?

"I'm ... I dunno," he shrugged.

They laughed even harder, teeth glinting like knives, and pinned him next to a Lincoln poster in the hall.

"You told Miss Conners you were *The Professor*," goaded the taller one with a smile like Catwoman's.

"I... she said it was a good answer," he told his sneakers. In class he had announced: "They call me *The Professor*."

"You're a *professor*?" snickered the less tall one, "and you got a *C* on the cell worksheet?"

He withered beneath their Siamese-cat gazes, but took hope when he saw Pee Wee approaching with two friends. "Hey Pee Wee!" he called in desperation. A kind word from the cool kid would set him free.

But Pee Wee was *Gordy* away from the block. "*Pee Wee*," one friend chortled. Pee Wee, now Gordy, flashed rodent teeth at Mikey. "What do you want, *Dick Head?*" He punched his friend and led him on a chase down the hall.

Solace was found at home in brownies warm and soft and sweet as his mother, who looked askance when he reached for a second—then softened her look when his eyes pooled with shame. "Have some milk," she sighed. Milk was good, there was no harm in that. It was homework in the kitchen each day after school, two brownies with milk, and no more than two—she drew the line there. He accepted her terms with a sly smile. His belly, face and thighs all rounded like dough. "My Pillsbury Doughboy," she said with a grin both loving and mocking. She jabbed at his belly, and he slapped her hand and knocked over the milk glass, flooding the table and soaking his pants. The next day the incident went unspoken. Two brownies with milk, and she ate brownies too as he did his homework. They dipped them in milk, compared milk mustaches, blew bubbles with straws, played follow the leader with fingers fast-walking through trails of crumbs. A little more time, and her body softened too.

Dad noticed. Was mute. Kept it inside for a day, several months, and then he burst, "What's with the damn brownies?"

"Michael's learning to bake," she reflexively lied. "It's a good thing, to bake. Cooking's useful for boys. Like on cookouts."

"Cookouts." They had never had cookouts. He waved her away with the back of his hand, trudged vexed and defeated back to his den—his principal reason for buying the house.

She gazed at her son in silent communion. He scrunched his brow to mirror her gaze, and she burst out laughing. The baking lessons began the next day.

A plump kid at his high school had very few options. His tenth-grade friends, two, were geeks before geeks were cool, and they strangled each school day with corrosive jibes at themselves and each other, then scurried relieved to the safety of home. His home reeked of smoke, for his mom had lost weight and smoked instead, and exercised, hacking, in front of the tube, compliant with Jack LaLanne's kindly commands.

"I'm gonna make lamb chops tonight," he said on the landing of the sunken living room. She sat in her leotards, spread-eagled before the TV, gazing up with ineffable longing at LaLanne in his snug workout suit, his curly hair mop and crinkly smile. "Lamb chops," he repeated, letting his head droop. She turned to him but did not seem to see. "*Lamb chops,*" she murmured, as if mouthing a prayer she no longer believed. Her blue eyes sparkled beneath pooling tears, and he thought them the loveliest eyes in the world, he thought her the most beautiful thing in the world. She blinked; tears cascaded. He wished to run to her to kiss her face dry, but stood rooted as if at the edge of a pond. She reached out willow-branch arms, but he would not venture into the pool.

He avoided his father whenever he could, not easy to do in a three-bedroom rancher. He craved a TV, Dad exploited the craving: "Tell you what. Bring me A's in math and science, and it's yours." An A in Chem but a B in Geometry. Dad pressed his advantage: "How's about we finally work off a little of that excess poundage, champ? Lose ten pounds by July, and we'll get you that tube. Fifteen, maybe."

He ate diet meals from the Weight Watchers cookbook with his mother for a month. They watched TV while snacking on roasted salted mushrooms and whole wheat toast topped with warmed cottage cheese and cinnamon. One night he folded a chocolate-covered cherry from his secret stash into her hand. She was intent on her program, didn't notice at first, then opened her palm and flung the contraband cherry away like a spider. "Don't do that, Michael!" Three cigarettes at last calmed her down. Two days later the weigh-in came. He rigged the scale and got the TV.

He watched summer TV reruns and news with his proto-geek

friends, one gangly, one plump. They hee-hawed at the world while feasting on treats that he prepared each night from his birthday cookbook: stuffed mushrooms, steak tartare, deviled eggs, and, one night, for a tea party lark, white-bread sandwiches with the crusts cut away. They put on British airs and erupted into hysterical cackles that pleased his mom in the living room but irritated his dad in the den. He was slicing olives for an encore round of sandwiches when the gangly friend, Ted, flounced to his side and said in an emergent baritone, "These are just *divine*, darling." Michael had to use the back of his hand, still clutching the knife, to wipe the tears that pooled in his eyes. His father appeared, and Ted flew like a leaf back into Michael's room. Michael looked up at his dad full of joy.

"Your friends are weird, Michael."

No movement save a tightening of stubby fingers on the slicing knife and a rapid dissolution of his gaze into darkness. "You are," he said.

The plump one, Eugene, was soft in spirit and body alike. It was he who remained when the summer got long and Ted tired of watching the world on TV: soldiers wading through rice paddies, hippies protesting out on the streets. Ted had gawked at comely protesters in fringed leather vests revealing flat bellies, and had followed them out onto the streets with no plan. Eugene remained content to cocoon. The two sat on cushions on Michael's bedroom floor and leaned back against the bed like a pair of young rajahs. Sometimes they'd doze. "Keep the door open," Michael's father admonished, "it's an oven in there." Or they'd lean against each other, arms melding like dough. "I said *open*," Dad snapped, then faded away for the rest of the summer.

They sent him away to college to broaden himself. Michael's dad set him up to rush his old fraternity, but he wandered the streets of Berkeley instead: incense, flyers, bookstores, bums. With two days left in Pledge Week, Dad cancelled *a big meeting* to fly up and drive Michael in silence to the frat house, and sat in the car watching his son trudge up the stone steps all the way to the door. Dad pulled strings, and the frat let him in. Although he had been forced upon them, and although short and soft, he was accepted provisionally: for when they'd venture to Telegraph, conspicuously frat boys, he was quick with terse quips to fend off street-people's jibes; and when they were drunk and couldn't count change, he'd figure tips and settle bills neatly. They first called him *Doc*, then *Beaver*, then *Scuzz*, but none of these stuck. Then Keith, a querulous jock leader, dubbed him *Chuck* with a wink over beer. Although it was senseless it sounded okay, for he didn't know that act followed name: Late at night, after the first big house party of the year, Keith and some others who had been denied flesh drank hard on the deck. Keith pointed his cleft chin at Chuck, and his minions pinioned Chuck's arms behind him and pulled his head back and pinched his nose and opened his mouth to a river of beer. They held his head up and the countdown began. "One small step for man," joked one when Chuck stood up with the vague idea of walking to the bathroom. Chuck doubled over as if shot, gushing vomit, and fell onto the deck semi-conscious. The vile muck pooled under his cheek. One guy placed a laurel wreath on his head, and a sympathetic soul draped a blanket over him when no one was looking. Three days later Michael pulled the washer's discharge tube from the drain-pipe before fleeing the house.

Michael took an apartment off campus with a slender English major who peered at him as if he were Raskolnikov, right there in the pad for his personal amusement. The English major, Robert, was beloved of Noreen, a fellow English major as pale as a veal calf who considered Robert an intellectual giant, mistaking assertiveness for inspiration. They grazed on hors d'oeuvres that Michael created, clutched his ladyfingers like cigarettes at the cocktail parties they foresaw attending. They allowed Michael to listen in to their erudite chats, and one night, after several weeks, they even allowed him to chime in beneath Robert's indulgent Freudian gaze and the soft gaze of Noreen, whose kindly affect clutched at his heart and sent him to the bathroom to hyperventilate. Michael's desire for Noreen showed in his clumsy efforts not to stare at her, and she intensified his longing with tender comprehending looks. Robert comprehended too, and derided Michael as *Robert Cohn* and *Holden Caulfield*, and alluded unsubtly while drinking gin to *The Lord of the Flies'* Piggy, and Ratso Rizzo, before punishing Noreen, Michael, and himself with contrived noisy sex sounds broadcast to Michael's adjacent room.

He took a studio in the flatlands of Oakland and stared at matches burning down to his fingers. He had only a hot plate, and lost fifteen pounds. Walking through Sproul Plaza at Berkeley, its antiwar and civil rights rallies, and leaflets and petitions for every left-wing cause, his underdog's heart drew him to the Young Republicans table where a girl with a bouffant Trisha Nixon-do stood flag-carrier tall as a pack of hissing leftists maligned her. He joined The Young Republicans on the spot and fell for the girl, who was well groomed, forthright, and knew what she wanted, and looked at him with princess eyes entreating rescue from a lonely castle. He licked envelopes under her supervision despite the bitter taste of the glue and his distaste for Nixon, which he kept well hidden—and his puppyish constancy wore down her resistance. Many nights they made out on the couch, until one night she joked acidly that a well-known Democrat was a secret "fag"—the word the bullies had flung at Eugene. He allowed dismay to enter his eyes, and she stared as if suddenly apprehending a roach.

He disappeared back inside his studio bunker with his burning matches and matching dark music, and ate SpaghettiOs straight from the can, three cans at a time. He studied sometimes, and sometimes wandered Telegraph as silently as a monk, wearing a grin that implied *he knew*. One midnight he walked the cold streets of Oakland beneath an overpass as if daring muggers. He returned home excited, yet disappointed somehow not to have been beaten. His mother called often, in a shrunken, frightened voice. He would search in vain for the power to speak. She'd call again and he'd let it ring while a match burned down towards his fingertips, determined not to blow it out until it stopped ringing. But his mom rang and rang, and he burned his fingers badly. He wrote jagged poetry, struggled to complete five sit-ups, cut the phone cord with a kitchen knife and poured himself into letters to his mother that he cut up and burned.

His hero sis, Jill, rushed down from Oregon and drove him up north in her yellow Bug. He begged her to drive the long way, through the coast redwoods, and those were the last words he spoke, which was okay with Jill. "Never you mind," she said with a lilt she'd acquired since leaving southern California. He stared out the passenger-side window with a strange humorous expression as they wound beneath the redwoods that enfolded them in parental shadows.

Jill shared a house with four young women studying theater at Southern Oregon University in Ashland, home of the famed Shakespeare festival. She prepped her roommates, and they spoke softly when he came out of Jill's room three days after arriving, calling him *Jill's famous brother*, *M'lord*, *Master Michael* and suchlike so as not to affright him. He sank into their soft thrift-shop couch and cradled his warm mug, and they allowed him to be himself, and to partake of them being themselves: hopeful, worried, nurturing, candid. They poked him sometimes with kind, curious eyes.

"I need a job," he squeaked in two weeks. Jill found him a job at a preschool serving university parents. The kids considered him a kid for his shortness and softness and because he spoke in a voice that was soft except at story time, when he'd become a whiny toad, a gruff kindly bear, a know-it-all owl or a flummoxed giraffe, with such conviction that they crawled up close to stare at his lips to see if he really, truly was human. One girl padded onto his lap, then the rest of the animals clambered up too, each forcing another kid off the cliff of his knee. The owner of the preschool, Janey, stared down at him with some apprehension: she had checked his background and found no problems, but what to make of this strange, shy creature who smelled of cookie dough and cried so convincingly as a baby elephant that a girl pressed a tissue to his glistening eyes.

Miss Miranda Plum, a young would-be elementary school teacher, was drawn to him too. She became his kitchen apprentice. Head down over his workspace like a boy preparing to launch a toy rocket, he taught her to make golden wafers encrusted with sugar crystals, and "Janey Fingers," and "Michael's Famous Brownies," as Miranda called them—all from scratch and all delightful, though he made the brownies just twice a month, for his hips still carried excess from his boyhood. To teach Miranda his secrets he had to speak sometimes, but most of the time he mimed his instructions, sometimes unfolding in mock comic confusion like Charlie Chaplin being mistaken for a baker and pressed into service baking for a king. Pressed against on all sides by kids as soft and sweet-smelling as cookie dough, he mimed comic surrender and allowed them to tackle him and crown him with a baker's hat they had spangled with arts-and-crafts cookies.

On weekends Miranda took him to a shadowed glade in the woods, a secluded fern dell, a clear river collecting the late summer chill. She pointed toes downward and plunged into the water, and he followed suit with a splayed, foot-first jump that scattered sparrows and squirrels. His dam burst in hysterics of wild forest howls, and her eyes saw him as a vision of nature. She apple-bobbed to him and they whirled in the water, bobbing, spinning, clinging, squeezing. They enclosed each other, he dove into her essence, fell into her *Baby!*, her baby, her own.

Iris Descending

The overtopped bathtub was science at its best, my dad's Bill Nye riff.

I wore a swimsuit, Dad lent me his goggles, and Mom set towels down at the edge of the tub. But I still hesitated. Can I really do this? They gave each other that look that said, Isn't she quite possibly the *best* eight-year-old in the history of eight? Sure, hon! said Dad. In you go, sweetie!

So in I went. Plop! And up went the water over the edge, bubbles foaming like breakers. Now you see, hon? That's how it happens! The ice melts—that's *you*—and flows into the ocean. And the sea level rises!

Why they were smiling, I couldn't imagine. Wasn't that why the polar bears drowned? Hadn't we just watched *Planet Earth* on Ecology Night—not some cheesy school event called Ecology Night, but our family Ecology Night, eating Chinese take-out and watching ecology shows? Had they forgotten the exhausted polar bear desperately swimming in search of an ice floe? Or me crying my eyes out, and starting a kids' club the very same night to end global warming?

I had to tune these people out. So while they beamed down at their anointed one, I became Ariel, splashing and thrashing, hiding from Ursula. Hm, I thought, this mermaid tail's handy! I thrashed my tail and splashed them all over. Dad wiped the foam from his eye with a humorous expression that said "Girls will be girls," but Mom probed my intentions with narrowed eyes. So I dove down for pearls.

"Still," said Uncle Gordon, my Chinese mom's brother, "your method is a proven success." We had the same conversation at Sunday restaurants for years—Uncle Gordon and Auntie Christine politely saluting my parents' success with their freewheeling American educational approach, my father, a white guy, basking in their approval, my mom looking down with lingering doubt. For the most part she went along with Dad's ways, for he had a good tech job, a mad-merry look that implied he knew something, and besides, unlike her, he was native to this land. But Mom's bones needed the Chinese approach.

So when we pulled up to the school for the first day of summer camp, she turned to the backseat projecting wisdom. "You must jump from hard ground if you want to rise high!"

I opened the door and trudged into Rise High. I mean, "Rise High!" We started camp each day with that cheer. Every morning, two hours of math, one hour of grammar, then out to the blacktop for organized tag. After lunch, it was computer lab and sustained silent reading. Then finally, near three, they'd plop us down with a few broken crayons, some gummed up gel pens, and a basket full of odds and ends.

I drew lovely hot air balloons or crafted funky ones from the bits in the basket. Balloons were my passion up through eighth grade. I imagined rising high above the city, looking down on the greenery of Golden Gate Park, then at the ocean where Ariel lived, then down at my school and the "average kids," as Mom and Dad called them.

The balloon obsession began in my toddler years. Dad painted my walls with a soft blue sky with multicolored party balloons rising up in the air, laughing kids hanging onto their strings. The balloons were near the top of the wall, and I would jump to catch the strings. The game started the night we watched *The Wizard Of Oz*, when I stood by the TV pretending to jump into the Wizard's hot air balloon. Dad's grin bounced as he jumped alongside me, and Mom looked on with a benevolent smile, just outside the circle of fun. *Jump The Basket* became part of my bedtime routine.

The other part was *Hot Air Balloon*. Dad would hoist me while Mom made the whooshing sound of hot air, and in Dad's arms I'd sail through the house high above a tropical rainforest, savannah, desert, and ocean. After touring the world we'd return to my room, and Dad would lift me up to touch the golden-winged Iris flying along the arc of the rainbow he had painted above the door frame while Mom whispered, like a soft breeze, "It's Iris ascending."

Iris ascended through the first half of childhood.

44

I got a smattering of A's in fourth grade, mostly A's in fifth and sixth, then all A's in seventh and eighth after private tutors, after-school programs, and two summers of Rise High! fixed my flaws.

I achieved "adequate progress" in violin in sixth grade, made second-chair in seventh, then switched to cello in eighth and made first-chair following twice-weekly lessons and daily two-hour practices throughout the summer. This was a career move by Mom, supported by Dad—I was the only cellist in school.

I earned honorable mentions in freestyle in fourth and fifth grades, bronze medals in backstroke in sixth and seventh, then gold in the breaststroke in eighth after switching at the urging of Mom and Dad both. "Better to be a big fish in a small pond," Dad smiled. Mom employed her accountant's mind. "Your chance for the Olympics are much better with the breaststroke, for sure."

I hated the breaststroke. It was too slow by far, and I hated sticking my head up when I swam. Freestyle was okay because I went fast, but even that felt like fighting the water. I loved swimming underwater, cocooned in the cool gelatinous flow, immune to the human noise up above. I explored undersea grottos, played with Ariel and her hip mermaid friends, swam with pods of dolphins. I loved the water, and the water loved me.

I quit, I told Mom towards the end of eighth grade. I was dripping with water, a just-won gold medal hanging from my neck. Her mouth opened, but no sound emerged. My mother had a lovely reserve, and an innocent sorrow that fascinated and gratified me. The breaststroke is dumb! I hate it! Too slow!

But you're good at it, she said in a deflating voice. I folded the medal into her hands. I dove in and flowed underwater half the length of the pool, then rose to the surface and gulped hot bleachy air. I dove down again and swam underwater to the far end of the pool, hoisted myself up onto the deck and climbed the high board. From the heights I saw Mom drifting out of the hall like a cork on the tide. I stepped to the end of the springboard, sprang high, dove, and sliced into the water, streamed down and curved up in a long rainbow arc.

My high school years were all underwater.

I chose Hades for my freshman English project despite Mom and Dad's suggestion of my namesake sky goddess. Dad mulled the crazy idea and said: "You know what, hon? Go for it!" My mother arched a dubious brow. But when I brought home an A, she quietly nodded. Then, in the park on a warm day in spring, I wrote a poem comparing the pressure for grades to the torment of Sisyphus, who never enjoyed a moment of rest though he strained to complete the same pointless task over and over. It was published in the school lit mag, and I felt perverse and strong when I showed it to Mom. She smiled bravely, but no words emerged.

Dad bought me a Fast Pass as a reward for my 4.0 in freshman year. "Independence is an essential life skill," he winked. "I don't mind driving her," Mom said with a gasp, contemplating the manifold disasters that could befall me on public transit or out in the town. "Too late," I said, snatching the pass and bounding down the steps.

It was the subway for me, not buses—too airy. I spent four whole weeks riding light rail beneath Market Street, too scared to go above ground, but sufficiently excited by life on the train. A filthy man swaddled in layers of dingy clothing stood over me. He was partly white, partly black, and partly something else, and somehow his skin was orangey in hue. A fly flew from his dreadlocks. The man gazed at the fly in wonder, and looked down to share the wonder with me. I returned his smile, and he sat down next to me. I used all of my swimmer's lung power to hold my breath to not smell his stink or show my disgust. When my lungs were ready to burst I turned my head to the side as if swimming the crawl, and puffed out quickly and sucked in quietly so the man wouldn't notice. But he noticed: for when he asked me for money, his smile was angelic; and when I laid two quarters into his big, dry palm, he called me *Calypso*. On the train I was noticed by high-school boys, and even grown men. That thrilled me and scared me, and I took care never to look their way twice. I studied tired old Chinese women toting pink plastic grocery bags, and young

46

adults in suits listening to iPods, and cute white boys with guitars, and ragged backpacking couples not much older than me looking weary but happy. I imagined their adventures on the road.

I introduced my bestie, Melly, to the underground, and she loved it in a horror movie way, clutching my arm the whole time we rode. We called ourselves The Rat Pack, and wore rat masks on Halloween that we wore later on Haight Street. Mom was philosophical. "Many Chinese emperors were rats," she noted. "It's a leader and conqueror, with a practical mind." She pointed to her own practical mind. "Rats rise to the top."

"Or run through the sewers," I said. "They brought the plague, Mom. Half of Europe died."

If I had not just earned an A in World History, she might have erupted. Not that she ever had erupted; but I thought of Mom as a dormant volcano, and felt that my high grades released the pressure that constantly pushed against her calm surface.

Melly's mother blew up a lot. Try as she might, Melly couldn't write well, and each B or C in English was a family crisis. "Be more like Ariel!" Mrs. Lin yelled. So I met Melly down on "B Street," deliberately blowing our final English essay in the first semester of sophomore year with misstatements like Hamlet was the Prince Of Norway, and Ophelia handed poison ivy to Claudius.

"You're a idiot!" Melly yelled when our grades came. "You could go to any college! Don't you know what that means?"

"I just want you to love me," I said.

She loved me, she must have, because she kept seeing me secretly even after her mom warned that Iris was dragging her down, and we'd both end up poor, like her cousins in China—like my mom's cousins, too. I had switched from violin to cello because Mom thought I would not make first chair, but Melly had stuck with it since third grade and was really good. It took her just three days to learn a bunch of pop songs to play while I sang and strummed underground at the Powell Street Station. I took up songwriting and wrote two dozen songs in just one summer, songs of peace and justice and love, and romantic songs, too. I made a few bucks and hundreds of flash-friends. One time a cluster of six or seven people stood listening, loving our music. Dad happened to walk towards us just then with a friend. How proud he must be of his free-spirited girl! But he turned a weak grin from me and walked on.

Why didn't you stop? I asked later, trying to sound cool.

He turned his gaze halfway from the computer screen, halfway to me. Pop music's fine, he said—then hesitated, as if composing his words, or considering whether to say them at all. But it doesn't help you get into college.

No, I said. You're right about that. And I flitted to the door, banging my shoulder against the jamb.

Dinnertime became increasingly gray as high school moved on. Mom ate gazing downward, and Dad's mood sank along with my grades. When he tried, on occasion, to revive the ebullience of my childhood years, Mom's face hardened as if ebullience were the problem.

Dad plodded into my room one night. I'm surprised at how your grades have fallen. These are yours, he said with a tired half smile, pointing at silver strands in his beard.

Dad, I said. What do you do?

He lifted his chin as if I'd struck him. I'm a programmer, he said. A techie. You know that.

I know, Dad, I said, but what do you do? Build schools? Save whales? Make music? Solve problems?

Yes, he said with hard dignity. I solve merchandising problems, Iris. I facilitate the delivery of product.

I nodded. We need products delivered.

I had turned seventeen just three days before.

Dad held his palm out in front of his mouth and mentally placed me onto his palm.

As if I were a ladybug, he puffed me away.

Emerald Beauties

The iniquities of the father are visited on the children to the third and fourth generation of those who hate g-d, our minister said. In the buckboard Aunt Em explained what *iniquity* meant, and I felt so proud to learn such an impressive word, for I was still small, Little Dottie they called me. I believed everything the minister said, but this particular warning meant little to me, for my uncle had taken me by the shoulders after I arrived and said quite plainly that although we were family I wasn't his child, but only his niece. His child, he said, was with the Lord now. It wasn't the lessons from those Sunday sermons that stuck with me anyway, it was the warmth that filled me when I thought of g-d's love, and the infinite mercy of the lamb of g-d.

We had lambs on the farm. They grazed in the tall grass, and in the springtime they bounced like cotton balls among the bluebells and purple coneflowers I'd gather for Aunt Em. And I'd bounce with them. I was knee high to a grasshopper, as Aunt Em said, so no one could see me in the tall grass. When we got tired, and the sunflower sun beat hard down upon us, the lambs and I rested beneath the twisted old apple tree in the middle of the alfalfa field, the only shade tree in that part of the farm. I cuddled the lambs and nursed them from a bottle. When Aunt Em made me stop, saying, quite correctly, that it would put them off their feed, I put my finger in their mouths and felt love flowing through me like milk.

One day Uncle was setting fence posts as I cuddled the lambs. He wiped the sweat from his brow and said with a voice that he failed to make soft that I should get back to work. Aside from working in my ABC primer, my work consisted of tending our kitchen garden, fetching water, and helping Auntie however I could. I obliged my uncle because he was right, and he hadn't asked for my mouth to feed. There was much work to do, for the field hands—we had had three hands for years, since right after the war, when prices were high—had lit out for better pay. "Greener pastures," Auntie explained with a sad patient sigh. Her words confused me because our pasture looked so lovely and green, a sea of tall grasses that waved at me in a personal way. I had felt betrayed because the men were my friends, but Auntie explained that you couldn't blame them, we were behind in their wages and had been often, and they'd stayed with us as long as they could. Judge not, Little Dot, lest ye be judged. I knew she was right, and repented of my pride.

A year or two later, Auntie and Uncle sat in the glow of the oil lamp and in low worried voices spoke cold words like *foreclosure* and *bankrupt*. Uncle tightened his fist around the fruit jar that held his apple jack, and Aunt Em touched his hand as if to say not too much, dear Henry, though she never would chastise him out loud.

It had long been her custom to call him *Dear Henry*, but she had done so mostly in earlier years, and in lighter moods. When Uncle matched her light mood he'd sing, "How shall I fix it, dear Liza?" Little Dot in those years would act out the song with a real wooden bucket, and we'd laugh as if our home was the whole world and a wonderful place. These days Aunt only brought *Dear Henry* out as a tool.

Uncle Henry had fought in the war, and Aunt Em told me he'd been a doughboy. On the porch on summer nights she'd tell me about the church social where he first spoke to her. He was the handsomest thing, she said, a tall Kansas boy just back from the war, and in uniform, too. He turned all the girls' heads. His hair was golden like corn, and his eyes were alight with goodness and truth. She said that he was a good Christian boy, a hard worker, and played "The Tennessee Waltz" on his grandfather's cornet. I clung to that image as the years passed. Uncle refused to talk about the war although I begged him to do so, so Auntie talked to me as we put up fruit. It's a hard thing to fight against evil, Dottie. It sneaks into men's hearts, it sneaks into their homes like the winter wind through the chinks in the timbers. Life is a battle of good against evil, and fighting evil is the Christian thing to do. There is simply no choice. Sometimes on Sundays she'd play "Onward Christian Soldiers" on the broken-down piano in our parlor, and she'd sing as loud and clear as she did in church, when I

50

was so proud to sit next to her.

"War's fine for them's never fought 'em," Uncle Henry said in a hard bitter voice the one time he ever did speak on the subject.

When I was still Little Dot, I couldn't stop thinking about how Uncle had been a doughboy. And from the time I was tall enough to reach the kitchen counter, when I was about four, until I was seven, my little girl's imagination told me that Uncle Henry must have been a baker in the war. I imagined him baking pies and bread for the brave Christian soldiers that fought The Hun as I helped roll out the dough for the apple pie we made from that one apple tree in the alfalfa field, or the Granny Smith trees in the back orchard.

There was more talk of bad prices from overproduction, and when I was ten we sold the piano and Auntie's walnut washstand. Again fearful words were uttered at night: *Foreclosure. Bankruptcy.*

Uncle borrowed from kin though it killed him to do so, and sold all our stock and the rest of our good furniture except my mother's bureau, because Auntie Em crossed her arms and said, Over my dead body. Uncle glared at her and she clutched her heart. I worried because I knew what a heart attack was, because Aunt Em had told me that Mr. Burnham, who grew wheat, corn, rye, and seven kinds of apples, including two that he'd cultivated himself, had died of a heart attack. Years later I learned that he shot himself rather than see his farm go. Uncle took every cent and bought a Fordson tractor and a combine like the big outfits with absentee owners that were taking over good land all over the county, outfits that plowed the tall grass under and cut down the fruit trees and farmed only corn, or only wheat, and nothing else. They loaded the last of our sheep onto a rancher's truck, and when uncle saw me crying he said, as he often had before, that we couldn't survive on the prices today. But he said it hard this time, with such a flinty stare at the horizon that I felt ashamed of myself for crying, and afraid of him.

He cleared the land in no time, it seemed, and plowed the alfalfa under to make more room for corn, and cut down the shady apple tree because it was in the way. Anyway the lambs were gone.

His first corn harvest was good, and he made good money—
cabbage, he called it. After the harvest he cleared the Granny Smith
orchard. The second harvest was good and the next ones were too, all
the harvests were good for years, and Uncle never let a field go fallow.
It's like printing money, he said, as green as the corn. You wouldn't
stop printing money, now, would you? I received a new dress three
times a year. There was nowhere to wear them excepting church,
however, for most of our neighbors had sold out to the large outfits
who could afford the machinery they could not afford. But I treasured
a necklace that Uncle bought in Kansas City, a genuine silver necklace
with a perfect ruby pendent cut into a heart. I looked at myself from
every angle and in every pose. At first Auntie sighed, and then she
railed about vanity in a shrill, desperate voice. But I didn't care.

The corn stalks stood tall in perfect green rows, and I walked
among them to be cool in the shade and to think about life when the
change came upon me. I danced among the rows at times, and
sometimes I cried for no reason at all. The corn stalks were my friends,
which was lucky, for I had no friends besides one girl who lived a long
bike ride away, and one boy, an old friend, who was going through the
change himself, and looked at me in a hungry way that disturbed me.

Uncle paid off his kin completely after the third year's harvest,
including a bonus of interest that they tried to refuse. He bought more
land from the people who owned the farm next to ours, the Pearson's,
who had been in the county for four generations. They were stubborn,
Uncle said, because they refused to change with the times, and that's
why they went bust. Uncle bought a scrimshaw pipe in Kansas City
and puffed on it with a satisfied look as he worked accounts late at
night. Auntie prayed for humility, but did so softly so that Uncle would
not think she was praying for him. Nor did she object when he drank
store-bought rye, but prayed that he find moderation and thrift.

There were more massive harvests and plenty of money, and
Uncle would say "We're in the long green" the way he would tell folks
we were "in the corn," or the way another farmer might say "We're in
the rye." He hired men, and they slept in a bunkhouse and did not eat

with us. He added two large rooms to the house.

The rain stopped falling when I was fifteen. We got by alright though the corn was stunted, for there was half a harvest, at least, and besides, Uncle had set cash aside. I spent nights walking the corn rows looking at the moon, but I was not praying for rain, as Auntie supposed, I was simply wishing to be somewhere else. To be anywhere else.

When I was sixteen there was no rain again, and the wind stripped away the topsoil which had nothing to cling to, with the grasses plowed under and the trees all uprooted. We covered our mouths when we walked out of doors if so much as a breeze blew. The wind blew for days, and clouds of dust rose and blocked out the sun.

All the people gathered at the county seat and stared up at the sky. A farmer's wife with a pie-shaped face pressed her lips together and squinted at the sky. The dust was dark and covered the land. It's a plague of locusts, she said. It's end times, a man said through clenched teeth.

Strangers came to all the farmhouses in the next days and weeks. Bankers came, and sharpies representing the big landholders came. Some were sent off at the point of a gun, but mostly folks listened— numbly, without hearing. A preacher came spouting Bible verses. Repent before it's too late, he said.

We thought we could survive till next year, for Uncle still had money in the bank, and he could borrow more at a good rate using the land he'd picked up cheap as collateral. He even thought he might pick up more land, cheap, from our neighbors. He never should have said it out loud, for Auntie fixed him a glare as long and hard as any I'd ever seen her give out. To my surprise, Uncle jutted out his lower lip and stared back at her. Then he raised the store-bought rye to his lips—to get her goat, I supposed.

The winter was harsh, and a hard, dead silence ruled the house. The spring thaw came and Uncle worked the parched land. Auntie and I prayed for rain, but we knew it was hopeless even if it did rain, for all the good soil had blown away, and what remained was powdery and dead, having been worked every season without rest.

We made plans to move. Uncle still had some money and hoped to buy a farm in California or a ranch in Montana where his people came from. Dorothy, said Em, holding my hand, you'll always have a home with us. You know that, sweetheart. Yes, said Uncle. But there was a holding back in his voice, and I knew we were done.

I was not the only girl hobo, I met quite a few. I learned to jump a freight and never had so much fun in my life. I'd hold the grip iron and stand at the open door of a boxcar to feel the wind blowing back my hair, which I no longer wore in pigtails, but had grown out in waves. I learned to panhandle, and the men called me *Meal Ticket* because I could cadge a handout so well. I'd say, Could I have some for my three friends too, please, and the lady of the house would grumble at first when she realized she'd been worked, then she'd smile a little and fill three more brown bags—*nosebags*, we called 'em.

Men paid attention to me for other reasons, too, and that kept me on edge, especially at night in the jungles. I'd attach myself to some older man who seemed decent, but one time my protector pulled me into the trees, and I only escaped by grabbing a rock as I lay on my back and cracking his skull. I lit out in the darkness and walked until dawn and hid in a hay loft. The hay smelled like home, and I wept.

I hid for three days in the barn behind a stack of hay bales, eating raw goose eggs and stealing apple peels and such from the slop. At last I pushed on.

I got lucky right off. I met a boy my age who was good to me and would not take advantage. He was a farm boy from Nebraska with sky-blue eyes and straw-colored hair and he was wiry strong, and nobody bothered me when I was with him. The older hobos liked us, called us prom king and queen, and we had fine times telling stories around the fire, drinking whiskey, singing, playing cards. I dealt cards like a wizard and was admired for that. The men admired me for my drinking, too, for I learned to drink whiskey because it warmed me at night, and then I learned to like it for the other reasons. They whistled at how I could drink so much without getting sick. But I had bad dreams.

Many of the 'boes were factory men who came from the east when the factories closed. They were decent men, but not our kind. Our kind were farm folk who talked like us and feared the same g-d, and Jim and I naturally flocked to them. They were Okies and Arkies and Texans, or from Kansas or Nebraska, but the townfolk called all of us *Okies* when we walked dirty and ragged into their towns. So we all took to calling ourselves *Okies* regardless of where we had come from, to show that we were all in it together. "Dumb Okie," we'd laugh, except those whose teeth hurt too much to talk.

We freight hopped to Oregon at strawberry time and stuck around to work blueberries. The blueberry camp was a good camp for migrants for we got ten cents a bushel, and the foreman let us sneak berries when we pleased. Jimmy and I smeared our faces with berries one day for no reason at all, and when we kissed, we were one juicy pie. I got the runs awful, but the sores in my mouth improved from the vitamins in the berries. Then we moved on and picked hops for a while, and when the hops were in, we climbed up onto a bright yellow boxcar heading down south to California, for we had long heard stories of its endless green valleys.

We signed on to pick apples at a big ranch in Lodi which grew their own variety called Emerald Beauties. They were a little sour like our Grannies back home, but were sweeter and rounder and as big as baseballs. The tree itself had twisted, gnarled branches like the Granny, but the Emerald's branches were even stranger, very knobby and thick. I thought how strange it was that such beautiful apples set on such odd trees. The foreman let each picker have an apple on the first day—"compliments of Mr. Martin" he grunted in a way that was contemptuous, it seemed to me, of Mr. Martin, us, and even himself—so we could see the value of what we were doing. I closed my eyes when I took my first bite and let the juice trickle down my neck. The foreman, a huge man called Pulaski, had a long broom handle that he used to knock apples, and when I opened my eyes he was pointing the stick at the juice on my breastbone and leering. Jimmy pushed the stick away in a clever, innocent way, as if the stick was a turnstile and he just wanted to pass. Pulaski's eyebrows were thick and black and had white hairs that stuck out like feelers, and he scrunched them together and glared down at Jimmy, but Jimmy played dumb.

Pulaski watched me all day. He made me climb up ladders to work the high branches, and I could feel his stare on my legs and my heinie. I was dizzy with anger that I fought to keep in, and got bees in my stomach. He watched me when I worked the low branches too because he knew my shirt would ride up when I reached. Jimmy hated Pulaski, and I called him son of a bitch beneath my breath. This added to my shame, because Auntie always preached that a good Christian girl never curses. Jimmy shot looks down at Pulaski from the tallest branches— Pulasksi always made him work the tall branches, and gave him rickety ladders. He also sent Jimmy on needless errands. One such time he walked up to me and pressed his stick lengthwise against my belly. Nice shape, he said. He said, I got a nice cabin, lots of good food. Chicken every day, and steak on Sundays. Red wine, table grapes, all the apples you could eat. Cheeses, almonds, every kind of olive. He knew I was hungry and longed for good food, apples most of all. We all longed for apples because we worked them all day but could not eat any, as eating them was a firing offense. Pulaski said he had a soft bed. You need a man, he said with a dumb, floppy smile, not a boy. I looked up into his stubbly face. If you touch me I'll kill you. My heart was knocking against my ribs, but I did not waver. You must always fight evil. There is simply no choice. His eyes grew large and his chest heaved, but he had no wit, and he stalked away.

I dreamed of apples that night. Not for the first time. I dreamed I was eating apple pie at the kitchen table with Auntie after supper, just we two. She was weary but happy, with that mild smile that comes from true goodness. Auntie Em, I said, and reached for her hand—but she vanished into vapor. I awoke from the shock in the darkness of the bunk house with cold sweat on my brow and strange women sleeping all around me. I bit my lip to stifle my sobs. My stomach growled. I spied a hunk of cheese the size of a bar of soap sticking out from beneath the pillow of a girl in a lower bunk. I thought for a moment of swooping down to swipe it. Instead I slipped on my pants and wandered out into the orchard. There was only a sliver of moon, and I groped my way along a row of trees to a section I knew had not been worked yet. I felt as though evil beings were looking down on me from either side, but I knew it was just the misshapen branches of the Beauties reaching out in the darkness, and no apple tree was going to scare me after what I'd been through. I pulled an apple from the branch and bit into it with a crunch that I imagined could be heard for miles around, the night was so still. It was sweet and tangy, like the one apple they'd allowed us on the first day. I bit again, and the juice rolled down my chin. But I slowed my chewing since the pulp got mealy. It was a worm, a big one, and I spat out bits of worm and apple and worked the saliva to get the worm chunks out from between my teeth and from the gap where a tooth had fallen out months before.

The next morning I had to have apple, but I had to have it in the light of day. So when Pulaski barked out assignments I pretended not to hear and set out walking towards a row of trees at the far end of the orchard, for Pulaski was lazy and I did not believe he would walk out that far. Two other girls were working the same section, and I had to wait twenty minutes or so 'til their backs were turned. I reached for an apple—but just as I touched it, something whizzing cracked my hand such that I liked to pass out. It was Pulaski's pole. I howled from pain and Jimmy came running, and when he got near Pulaski whacked him in the forehead and Jimmy went down, a gash in his forehead pouring blood. She's a thief, said Pulaski, pointing at me with the pole, then he jabbed Jimmy in the gut with it. He tried to attack me, he told the pickers who were watching. There was a threat in his gaze, and they lowered their eyes. He looked down at Jimmy, who was trying to sit up. Blood was pouring from his head, and I pressed my scarf to his forehead with my good hand and forgot all about the pain from my broken hand for a moment. Five minutes, Pulaski growled. Five minutes, you're gone.

We worked our way by thumb and freight to the apple country

along the California coast north of San Francisco because the air was cooler than the San Joaquin Valley, and if we were going to starve, we might as well be comfortable. But with us looking more bedraggled than ever, and Jimmy with a big red scar on his forehead, the hiring bosses screwed their noses up as if we were troublemakers, even reds. Also, my busted hand was bound in cloth, and though I hid it behind my back, they always seemed to sniff it out. Literally, maybe, because it smelled rank. My whole self smelled rank. Also I had buried my hair inside a cap to look more plain in case I was hired and the foremen were pigs, and that may have also helped us not to get hired.

So we made our way to the Russian River and bathed in it to wash off the stink, and we swam around laughing and lay out on a sand bar. Then the hunger bit and we set off again. The sole of one of Jimmy's shoes was loose and flapped at the toe when he walked, and he said, what the hell's so funny about that, that they make those cartoons of hobos.

There was an orchard we found by following the marks left on trees by other 'boes before us. There must have been many because the orchard was posted all over with no-trespassing signs and fenced with barbed wire. We looked across the wire at an orchard of beautiful trees set with red and gold apples maybe two or three days shy of picking. We didn't dare go in to take apples in the daylight, so we followed a beaten foot trail down into a ravine and found a camp of ten or twelve 'boes lounging next to a little gully fifty yards from the orchard. They welcomed us but their eyes were dull, as if they'd been on the road six months too long. They gave us each a hunk of bread, and we knew not to ask where it had come from.

It was an Okie camp. All the men came out of the Dust Bowl like us, and all had the same story: the fruit trees uprooted, the grasses cut down, the soil never replenished, turned to dust in the wind.

Ye shall reap, the camp wit grinned, as ye shall sow.

We sowed like we knew, said a man bitterly. Like the big boys with the money. Folks got to keep up.

Never mind, brothers, another man said. He took up a rutted

guitar. We've landed in a better place, he said, and gazed grandly and facetiously up at the redwoods surrounding the gully. I followed his gaze to the tops of those majestic trees, the most magnificent trees I had ever seen. I walked my gaze all the way from the tree tops down to the beautiful undergrowth of spear-shaped ferns of a lovely light green. California is a Garden of Eden, the guitar picker sang, a paradise to live in or see. The men chuckled—some lightly, some bitterly—but they all knew the song. The guitar picker played until dark.

I'm getting some apples, Jimmy said. There was hardly any food, and the men hardly moved the whole time we were there. They were desperate to get hired in a day or two to knock down apples in the orchard nearby. I'm coming too, I said to Jimmy.

We used sticks to poke our way up the ravine to the edge of the farm and crept southward along the fence, then cut east at the corner of the field to the farthest point away from the house. It was warm and the air smelled of hay and horse dung. Jimmy had wire cutters from one of the men. He snipped the two lowest wires and in we crawled. There was a tree twenty feet in from the fence set with apples so big we could see their outlines even in the darkness. I reached for one but fell back onto the ground at the sound of a shotgun blast. Leaves and apples fell all around us. We ran back to the fence without looking back and scrambled through the gap in the wire. All I kept thinking was, don't shoot my heinie. A few feet on the good side of the fence we ducked behind a tree and looked back. We saw the dark outline of a man watching us. His legs were spread, and a shotgun rested across his shoulder. He had not shot to kill and did not wish to kill, but he had sure enough shooed us away from his crop.

Have fun? asked one man with a hard kind of laugh.

Sure, Jimmy said. A million laughs. His hand was pressed to his leg. I made him show me. It was bleeding from a barb that had torn a gash two inches long on the top of his thigh. I ministered to him with water and alcohol to clean the wound, then asked the men to let him have whiskey. When they saw how ugly the gash was, they passed it right away. Jimmy took one long swallow—moderation was his way—

then set his jaw while I stitched him up with catgut the way I'd seen Aunt Em do so many times for Uncle Henry and Zeke, Hunk, and Hickory, the field hands we'd had when I was small. I thought about them while I pulled the catgut through Jimmy's skin. I remembered Zeke pulling a splinter from my hand that I got climbing the fence around the pig pen. I got lost in my past, and Jimmy was somewhere else too, staring blankly across the gully as if he didn't care about the wound or the pain or anything else. I stitched the wound up pretty neatly and bandaged it with a cloth that a man from Texas pulled from his bindle.

A man played the blues harp. He played comically, with warbles in strange places and wiggly phrases, and breathy jerks where you didn't expect them, like a carnival ride. Some of the men laughed, and some didn't—or, as it seemed to me, wouldn't. The player put the harp down and looked with sad clown eyes at the men who weren't laughing. Here, sis, said a round man who was all balled up in rumpled clothing. He was from Broken Arrow, a for-real Okie. It's good for the soul, he said with a halfway sort of grin. It was whiskey, and his offer meant that I was okay. I paid him the country courtesy of not wiping the mouth of the bottle even though his mouth was juicy and his lip had a sore, and he acknowledged my courtesy by bowing his head like a gent. I took a huge slug and he raised his brow in appreciation of my prowess. Go on, he gestured, so I slugged some more, and the party resumed. The man with the harp commenced to play and the guitar picker joined him. I crawled over to Jimmy, set my face in his lap. He patted my hair, which was stringy but clean from bathing in the river.

I dreamed of apples of all colors hanging by the dozens like Christmas-tree ornaments on tall twisted trees in a deep dark grove. I reached for one but the tree was alive. It slapped my hand—my broken one—and I screamed in terror and pain. I bolted upright. Jimmy was asleep, as were most of the others.

An old hobo with a long craggy face was staring at me in an accusing way. He stabbed the air with a long gnarled finger. You have sown the wind, he said in a scratchy voice, ye shall reap the whirlwind.

He scrunched his nose, and darkness filled the furrows. You have sown the wind, and shall reap the whirlwind. He thrust his finger. My heart felt stabbed.

Manners, Rev, said the Texan.

The Rev still glared at me and I lowered my eyes. A tear fell like fruit.

Ashes to ashes, the Texas man said with a philosophic air. He picked up a handful of ash that had cooled. Dust to dust. He let the ash fall out of his hand. Ain't that the perfect verse for us, Kansas? For dust 'boes like us?

No sir, I said.

I couldn't look up, but I felt the men's hunger as I felt my own hunger growling inside me, and I smelt the stench of their unwashed bodies mingled with the sweet wood smoke. A skeeter stabbed my neck, and hordes of others lighted on the ashen faces of the sleeping men, disturbing their dreams. Flies buzzed Jimmy's wound. I was glad that I'd dressed it.

Iniquities, sir.

I impulsively covered my ruby pendent.

Visited on the children.

For Tink!

He was a quick-witted quipster with a distaste for the low or the mean. He was hipped to haiku, popped apt aphorisms, had an ear for idiom, carved clever couplets. He considered Hemingway's style ideal and had since tenth grade when the words "lean, athletic prose" on a book jacket elevated his vision. He said he felt elevated in class and was banged up hard against his locker. He took it the first time, but the next time lashed out and gashed a jock's nose, though it cost him a beating.

She consumed Victorian novels like luscious chocolates, had a goldfish named Brontë, had filled eight dozen journals from ninth grade through twelfth with lines that flowed and bent and dove and rolled on towards an unreachable sea. She founded Jane Austen Tea in high school and wore white opera gloves to every senior event, and her flaxen hair reached down to her shoulders without curlicue or other digression.

They met as English majors the first week at UCLA, when an aged professor moving beyond earthly cares recited Wordsworth in a cracked soaring voice. She caught the trail of a cloud of glory and laid one slender leg across the other as if it were an antenna calibrated to human emotion. He saw, and must have her body and soul.

In the library, in their dorms, then in their apartment, they read each other's favorites from fourth grade on for each other's sake. She, for him, read *Hatchet*—his first love—and *Where The Red Fern Grows, Treasure Island, The Lord of the Rings, The Call of the Wild, White Fang, The Sea Wolf*, and *The Catcher in the Rye*. He told her of the epic night he had spent alone in King's Canyon in sub-freezing weather at the age of sixteen after reading *To Build A Fire*. He had chopped wood with the cherished hatchet his parents had bought him when he finished reading the namesake book, and built a fire using the technique and materials employed by the doomed tenderfoot in the London story, keeping it burning while sipping hot broth through a ski mask. He had eschewed food to avoid tempting bears, and brandished a long, stout pine staff sharpened to a point, and gazed up at the multitudinous stars in the hard, deadly night. His account of the experience had won a school-district essay contest and helped him to college, where none of his low-income Fresno clan had ever gone before.

He, for her sake, read *Charlotte's Web*, *The Wind in the Willows*, *The Secret Garden*, *Peter Pan*, *Alice In Wonderland*, *A Wrinkle In Time*, *Harry Potter*, *The Importance of Being Earnest*, *Pygmalion*, and a three-course Brontë banquet. The sight of him lying peacefully on the couch with *Jane Eyre* in hand stirred a passion more fulsome than that enkindled by the sight of his lean body dripping ocean water when they'd journeyed to the beach with anthropological curiosity to observe the abnormally tanned natives of L.A. Sighing with ethereal pleasure, she wafted to the floor like a maiden spreading her dress on the green and laid her head in the crook of his arm. "Little Janet," he said, lightly brushing her hair.

Reader: "Janet" is Jane Eyre. Our girl is named Emmy. Our man is Jack Gardner.

"*Jack* is a notorious domesticity for *John*!" quipped Emmy in the fizzy flush of new love, "and I pity any woman who is married to a man called *John*." She had gone too far and both knew it, so they avoided eye contact—but electricity flowed through their intertwined fingers.

At last they arrived at their college reading lists. He, for her, read *Wuthering Heights*, offering no comment beyond an approving mention of Heathcliff the rogue, and *Middlemarch*, and *Pride And Prejudice*, and as much as he could of *Sense And Sensibility*. She read his twentieth century American lit with a mind newly opened to it for his sake. She respected Hemingway without affection, admired Steinbeck's compassion and compression, and liked Jack London, too, for she saw her Jack in him—although, in a peevish moment while tugging at her hair over a difficult composition on Henry James, she dismissed London as "a writer for boys." Jack stormed out without speaking, and as penitence, she refrained from touching a book for two days. When he returned she threw her arms around his neck, and he forgave her by saying nothing. This approach to conflict was new to her, for she hailed from a lively San Francisco family dominated by loquacious females who believed in talking things out, and she appreciated his stoicism, which she attributed with romantic license to the hard-baked dirt of his native Central Valley. So instead of proposing a heart-to-heart, she drove him to the hills of Topanga Canyon, where he laid her down in a thicket of trees.

He liked *The Great Gatsby*, and saw the title figure in himself. She recognized surface similarities—he was handsome, jaunty, restless, and ambitious—but discounted the related implication of unreliability, for as the college years passed he invariably rebuffed the English Department honeys who swarmed about him. And so, when they surfaced from a steamy kiss in the back alley outside a midnight Film Noir marathon on a drizzly night during senior year, and the streetlight shone on the glistening blacktop, he attempted to say a thing with a look, and she read the look and threw him a rope: "So whaddya say, ya big lug—wanna bag me?"

They wed in June in the Shakespeare Garden in Golden Gate Park, reciting self-written vows beneath a bower heavy with jasmine.

"No breath that I take, no lakeside walk on a gray afternoon, no romp in the sun, no warmth by the fire... no day, no elation, no hope, no dream—but you give it fullness, and you give it grace."

He answered: "Two hearts, one dream, one life, one love."

They honeymooned in Ireland, where they walked Joyce's Dublin and journeyed on a whim to Yates' Lake Isle Of Innisfree. Nine journals did she fill there with notes that would color her fiction one day. He encouraged her in this, recognizing in her a breadth of vision and a depth of feeling beyond his own, and he ceded the dream of writing to her. It had been his dream, too, in an unfocused way, but years of shredding by male T.A.s had torn his confidence, and he thought it wise to treat graduation as the time to make a clean break with delusions.

Back home they toured Hammett's San Francisco and London's Oakland, and made a pilgrimage to the Calavaras County of Twain to attend the Jumping Frog Jubilee. They found work right away, for it was the height of the dot-com boom, and joined the happy ranks of young English majors from all over the country being paid (paid!) to write (paid to write!)

"Write *content?*" she sighed, brushing her hair in the fog-gray mirror. "Did Shakespeare write *content?*"

"*Produce* content," he said, appreciatively gazing at her sleek nightgowned form. He framed a movie screen between his hands and spoke in that stentorian movie-trailer voice: "He was an Elizabethan playwright whose brilliant plays captivated king, queen, and country. All's well! And all seems apt to end well, too—until he is time-warped to a parallel world: San Francisco in the Internet Age! Will he raise the cultural level for all, or be dragged down into the muck of a debased epoch? *Shakespeare 2.0.* Ask thy mama to boot it up!"

"You'll be the king of content," she purred. She hoped to be the queen, for her start-up intended to be *thee* (they always, humorously, said *thee*) literary destination of Web 1.0 with book reviews, essays, fiction by notable authors, along with fiction by their own talented young staff, plus author interviews, plus... plus—well, they hadn't really determined what else they would do, and "plus... plus" became a catch phrase at work. They did, however, have five-million dollars in first-round funding and a lease on a brick warehouse South of Market in which they enjoyed foosball, ping pong, a pocket gym, and Webvan deliveries three times a week.

He worked for a site that was building a massive database of reviews of old films in the hope of enticing a corporate suitor. His reviews were perfect for the new medium since he cut to the chase and closed at two-hundred-fifty, or fifty words fewer than he was allotted.

"I've barely cleared my throat at two-hundred." She massaged her temples and considered for the fifth time the seventh draft of the first paragraph of the first short story she had been authorized to write for the site.

He popped a kernel of popcorn and fast forwarded past several scenes of a film he was reviewing for work. She arched her brow. "It's alright," he assured her with a roguish smile, "I just need the gist: the acting, dialogue, plot, sets, and costumes. Then I rate it from one star to five. It's all in the template." Her brow fell on *template*.

Her company folded when the chief funding angel turned off the spigot. "For failure to *monetize*," she said with an acid rendering of the neologism. Nor was her story ever pushed live, for at two-thousand words it was much too long for a website.

His firm thrived and he along with it on the strength of his productivity complemented by the charm and decency with which he neutralized rivals and made managers pliant. Particularly pliant was the managing editor, who touched him on the nape in the office one night and cooed *noble rustic* into his ear in a testing way. He rebuffed her but concealed his disdain, and this gallant note secured her admiration and increased his stock options. When the firm was acquired he earned thirty-five-thou from the options and bought his-and-her kayaks, hiking boots, a tent, and a convertible roadster.

She developed chronic headaches and indentations at her temples from the pressure of her fingers when moaning, "Why... why... why?!"

"You need to go hiking," he told her. She knew enough to take hold of Superman's cape, and he zipped her up to Napa in his snazzy new ride. They hiked Robert Louis Stevenson Park in the cold and followed the mist up to the site of the cabin where the author honeymooned in 1880. He apprehended the site with the uplifted jaw of a sea captain sighting a fabled land, then led her by the hand through an overgrown side path and laid her down in a redwood grove.

Three weeks later, in Sausalito next to the bay, he announced in that movie-trailer voice: "He was a noble savage from the hardscrabble streets of the San Joaquin Valley. She was a cultured queen from the fog-shrouded hills of the Cool Gray City of Love. They were high on love but low on money. And then: Hollywood called! CLOSE UP OF JACK, in his boxers, taking a call. Hello? Do *what*? For *how much*? Starting *when*? Yowza! FADE OUT. Narrator intones movie title and tagline: *Writing Trailers For The Big Bucks*. Because sometimes less can mean so much more."

"*Trailers?*" Her words hissed out through the tiny aperture formed by her lips.

"Not just trailers—so much more!"

She slumped against the seawall. "Like?"

He gently rotated her towards the water, rested his chin upon her head from behind, envisioned his future dancing on the bay. "Taglines," he answered. "And teasers."

Her voice, as weak as a dying fairy, was inaudible to him.

"I love you," he told the sprites dancing over the water.

Her solace was that there was no immediate need to move to L.A., a place she abhorred and which he had always said he abhorred too, for the marketing firm was parceling work out to him on a trial basis. He had landed the gig on his editor's recommendation to Evyn Of Beverly Hills, a PR heavy. He had admitted that he lacked copywriting experience, but Evyn assured him, "In this town, hon, it's all about talent."

"And sex appeal," said Emmy dryly.

They spent their mornings in the gray light of their drafty Victorian flat, she with her fingers curled high over the keyboard like a praying mantis forgetting how to strike, he on his back with eyes peacefully closed. Deep into a fruitless writing session she tugged at her hair as if to pull recalcitrant words out through the pores of her scalp. With great excitement he sprang to a sit: "How's this for *Frat House Freaks?*" He leaned back to decant his inspiration. "Full frontal crudity!" He smiled like a child who has puzzled out a difficult spelling. She massaged her temples and stared blankly ahead. "Hon?" he said.

"It ..."

"Needs work, I know."

She sought an elegant construction to challenge his premise that editing three words is "work," but no words came. "Guess my haiku experience is more practical than I realized," Jack marveled, settling back down on the couch with eyes pleasantly closed in anticipation of the Muse's next surprise. As Emmy gnawed her nails, bereft of inspiration and vexed by his, an impish grin signaled Jack's conception of another tagline.

"Hey," he asked over a huge sushi splurge to celebrate his receipt of a permanent offer, "did I tell you what they said about my Easter-movie tagline?" He had told her, twice, but she did not wish to say so, and stared like a teen cornered at Thanksgiving by a bombastic uncle. "For *Easter Bunny Rampage?*" He leaned back grandly. "*This time it's for Peeps!* In the agency they call it *the legendary Peeps line!*" Emmy said that's nice, or meant to, she wasn't quite sure: for many months, her voice had been shrinking.

He understood drama, there was no doubt of that, and he timed their arrival in L.A. to be a triumphal drive along the Malibu coast beneath a blazing June sun. Glimpsed through a squint with an untethered mind, the sun of L.A. was a blood-devouring Aztec god, and he gazed up as if at a brother deity while she stared fixedly down at her crossword. "Prescient, buying a convertible," he mused. "*Pre-sci-ent*," she said as if answering Sixteen Across. He nodded at the beach like Gatsby gazing at the beguiling green lights of Daisy's dock, and impulsively suggested a day at the beach. Her twisted grin registered disbelief: they had visited the beach only once during their four years in college, and then only in the ironic guise of anthropologists studying primitives. "I think a scene from *Farewell My Lovely* took place in those hills," he said for her sake, with a glance at the towering palm-crowned bluffs. "We should do a Raymond Chandler tour." The promise ignited a spark in her eyes. "And a Pynchon tour," he added. She brightened and murmured, "And a Didion tour. And *Day Of The Locusts*." She set down her puzzle and hiked up her knee, and her sundress settled midway down her thigh, which was not tanned like a beach bunny's, but bike-toned and shapely.

"It's a sexy town," he asserted, a promise in his words.

The feeling of a second honeymoon flavored their first summer in town, for his salary was high, the weather superb, and they had time to play. They rented a small apartment in Santa Monica a mile from the beach, and she set up housekeeping with extraordinary diligence, ignoring the nagging sense that she did so as an excuse not to write. There was money enough, she told herself, and everything had its season—and this was the season to enjoy the good life like Graham Greene in Cyprus, or the Shelley's in Italy. Leisure abroad feeds the writer's soul, she thought. At night, there were splashy restaurants and evening strolls on the promenade on the high bluffs overlooking the sea, and aimless drives with the top down exploring the region: she called it a *region*, never a *town*. In the mornings, while he worked, she assembled and lacquered prefab furniture, made handicrafts to decorate their walls and tables, created playlists to match the moods of the day (including their frequent amorous nights, so energized was he by his new life), stocked the kitchen with cookware and staples and spice jars that she labeled by hand, and prepared cold soups and curries. In the early afternoon, when the kitchen air was rich with savor, she read leisurely; in the late afternoon she read intensely, for Jack had lost his taste for cozy evenings on the couch with great books, and preferred going out every night—still with her, mostly, but once or twice a week with his fellow copywriters in a klatch they called *Le Talent* with one part irony and three parts ego.

She, however, lacked friends of her own, for she was carless and jobless and lost in the sprawl, and averse to the arid feel of the town. Because she was lonely, he invited her to have drinks with Le Talent. She sat packed in between him and four other young hotshots before a flotilla of tropical drinks, growing physically dizzy from their zinging one-liners, and morally queasy from their sexual innuendo about office personnel. In the fizz of the third round the talk turned to the "miracle of compression," as one bright young man called it, that was required to convey the essence of a film in a catchphrase, and a sharp young woman declared that an "esthetic of minimalism" governed their work. Jack read dismay in subtleties of his wife's expression, and slurred a couple of superficial references to haiku and senryu to make her feel better. Then Le Talent toasted *Love's contagious*, the firm's famed tagline for the smash film romance about a beautiful epidemiologist and a handsome working-class widower during a small pox epidemic started by terrorists. Reverent silence reigned. Emmy had scarcely spoken all evening, but yielded to the prompting of a tipsy inner imp. "I wonder," she mused in her most cultivated tone, "whether two words could capture both the ghastly horror and the often-overlooked humor underlying, say, The Holocaust? Or might it take three?" They studied her face for irony, malice, even self-deprecation—but her gaze and twee grin defied decoding. They looked at Jack because she was his doing, and he looked at her with the fond yet detached expression of one viewing the yearbook picture of a high school girlfriend whose appeal has since dissolved into wonder. She endured the rest of the evening in silence, jotting acid notes about Le Talent for future literary use on cocktail napkins decorated with colorful cartoons of bare-breasted Polynesian girls shaking grass-skirted booty.

September arrived with dry baking winds. Jack took to wearing white combed-cotton shirts with the top two buttons undone and a one-hundred-fifty-dollar pair of gold-rimmed sunglasses "to battle the beastie," meaning the sun. She called him "Ken" as he left for work, a trick of her mouth camouflaging her malice. But he knew her ways and perceived her intent, and registered it as a puzzle to solve later, not allowing it to slacken a smile which shone as brightly as his star at the firm. Perhaps, he thought, if he brought her deeper inside of his world? So he implored her to accompany him to a cocktail-do at Evyn's Hollywood Hills home in a development grandly called *Mount Olympus*. Leading her by the elbow past Evyn's shimmering blue swimming pool to the edge of the garden, he gestured wordlessly at the galaxy of silver lights stretching out far below as if he were Balboa overlooking the Pacific, or Moses beholding The Promised Land. She deliberately withheld the approbation he sought, and he wondered if she was a bit of a drag, more suited to her "provincial little burg," as his friends at the firm called San Francisco, than the powerhouse capital of the entire West Coast, which he—"The Strong Silent Seeker Of the San Joaquin Valley And Righteous Ribald Rustic" of drinking-game fame—took to so nicely. Or was she perhaps jealous of his talent and good fortune? Jack averted his eyes from her disquieting expression and lighted on a great eminence. Emmy followed his gaze to a jumpy little fellow with poodle-sized eyebrows who was cramming shrimp puffs into his mouth before three fawning acolytes. "It's the author of *Fission Trip*," Jack said with great consequence, referring to the then-ubiquitous pop-culture catchphrase from the ad campaign for a blockbuster romance between a whistleblowing Russian ballerina and a crusading American journalist running from the KGB after Chernobyl.

"*Author?*" she said with naked consternation.

He gazed past her at Evyn, slender and stylish in a low-backed black cocktail gown displaying the "fit, fabulous, forty-something frame" she boasted of, holding court before a sycophantic gaggle. "What?" he said, as if roused from a trance.

"You said *author*."

"No I didn't."

The shrimp puff tasted fetid in her mouth, like an uncleaned alimentary canal. She discharged it openly into a napkin.

One bleak November day, as Jack donned kid gloves while leaving for work, Emmy said in the sarcastic tone that increasingly salted her comments, "It's *cold* in Paradise?" After pushing the door shut behind him, she surveyed the apartment and realized in horror that she had furnished every corner, adorned every surface, and organized all of their possessions down to boxes of binder clips that she had divided by size and labeled in lovely calligraphic letters. Her horror derived from the disappearance of her excuse for not writing, but she suppressed that harsh epiphany for eight days by inventing compelling new calls on her time: procuring must-have spices for new must-cook recipes for Jack, for the sake of the marriage; volunteering at the soup kitchen, for it was, after all, the season of sharing, and she missed the soup kitchen she'd volunteered at back in San Francisco; and touring neighbor-hoods, jotting down physical details for descriptive passages for the fiction she would surely write, when she wrote. On the ninth day she looked at her unwashed hair in the mirror, took a great cleansing breath and sat down at her desk and wrapped her tea mug in fingerless gloves. She sat tugging at her hair all that morning. And all week. And for two weeks, and three. And nothing, but nothing ever happened. Week after week she gazed out the window at naked branches networked like dendrites, feeling their barrenness as her own.

She massaged her temples and her scalp: for in the hungover New Year's Day that followed a New Year's Eve of faked joy, she discovered a quarter-sized bald spot atop her crown, and hoped to stimulate regrowth. She rubbed the spot like Aladdin's lamp—but instead of a genie, conjured memories of the rapture she had once experienced editing Jack's college compositions for the love of Jack, the love of language, and the love of thought, as if midwife to Jack's inchoate ideas. So exquisite was the pleasure derived from ennobling Jack's prose that she had described it to a girlfriend, with measures of editorial and womanly pride, as quasi-sexual. Surely she would enjoy this still—and maybe, just maybe, it would bring them closer. But how to edit *Split happens*, Jack's career-building tag for the animated summer hit about a competition to build the world's greatest banana split? Or *Double, double, broil and bubble*, his well regarded tease for a Food Network program? Or *Only the young die good*, his award-nominated tag for a Jack Nicholson/Christopher Walken buddy pic about two unrepentant old reprobates who jettison their last remaining vestiges of social conscience in their declining years?

"I can't write," she said in bed with a penitential hush and a wide-eyed stare at the ceiling. "I'm blocked! Totally, thoroughly, permanently blocked."

"I know what you mean," he said, for he had just spent the evening on the couch with eyes closed, trying in vain to summon a tagline for *Loose Cannons III*. She turned with a wry smile anticipating his, but his earnest expression so lacked self-awareness that he clearly needed more help than she.

So she scattered books around the apartment like clues on the path back to Jack's old self. Whitman. Emerson. *Siddhartha. On The Road.* Biographies of Lincoln and Gandhi, Lord Byron and Van Gogh. All went unread, though he picked a few off the couch and the kitchen countertop, musing that the little place had grown cluttered, and they ought to upgrade if he got that promotion. She gazed at the sea and hinted with little hope of travel: Thomas Mann's Venice? The Lost Generation's Paris? Mark Twain's Missouri? "We've got the Travel Channel," he said, aiming the remote. So she shared stories of young Americans building schools in Mali, staffing medical clinics in the Andes, building homes for the poor in America. "Cool," he said, then closed his eyes to meditate on *Great Big Boobs*, the upcoming buddy pic about two big, dumb detectives going undercover as waitresses at a Hooters. She visited the Unitarian church, and told him of celestial music played by women in indigo saris, and of stirring sermons of love and peace. "That's nice," he allowed as if brushing off lint.

Resigned to defeat, for herself and for him, she joined a yoga class with the self-defeating expectation of L.A.-style yoga done for ego's sake, not yoga's. In the group she saw what she expected to see, artificially tanned, overly thin middle-aged women with loose arm skin and surgery-tightened faces whose eyes betrayed the terror of aging—a terror far more intense here than elsewhere. But she failed to notice an unadorned young woman much like herself, who sought a friend as she did herself.

She looked for work as a writer or editor, but did so in a desultory fashion, for the prospect of film or TV work appalled her. Jack looked over from the tube and was stunned by the wanness of her face and the deadness in her eyes; so he swallowed, twice, and offered to get her an interview at the firm—cautioning her, with brotherly solicitousness, that he wasn't entirely sure she was suited for the fast pace, or cut out to write with the needed compression. She gazed down at folded hands and mumbled phrases he could not decode, like a Salem maiden accused of witchcraft. Now his full attention was hers. And he didn't merely lower the set's volume, as he usually would, but turned the thing off, and stared at her with canine concern. She would not meet his gaze, but stared at her hands as if lifting her head was beyond her power. He placed a tentative hand upon hers, and she twitched as if Tasered. Her reaction stunned her as much as him.

"Tink's dying," she said in a small, tear-choked voice.

Jack jerked his head back like a punch-drunk boxer inhaling smelling salts. He shook his head to bring himself to, and lowered himself to her side on one knee.

"Tink's dying," she repeated in an oracular tone.

"Then let's save her," Jack said, and took her limp hand and puffed on it as if fanning a spark in kindling, as he'd done at sixteen in the freezing wind of King's Canyon when building a fire with shredded bark and a match. She choked off a laugh but squeezed his hand like a catatonic signaling her awareness of a friend's presence.

To take prompt action he canceled cable, then fixed her favorite herbal tea. She cradled her Brontë Sisters mug for some time before sipping. He draped a throw over her shoulders as if she'd been fished out of freezing waters, and sat at her feet with his head on her lap as dusk turned to night.

When she thawed she uttered tentative words that fluttered softly into the air. She dreamed, she dared say, of founding an online lit mag about keeping dreams alive. As editor, she would midwife writers' dreams. She turned to him for the first time all evening, knowing that the job just wouldn't get done without his boundless energy and resourcefulness. The idea flickered in the dim room, and he puffed it with a kind word and a smile. She revived more fully. And as he sat at her feet with his arms in her lap, she glowed with a light he had not seen for months. She streamed ideas all night, and he jotted them down. And by dawn, *Clap For Tink!* had been fully conceived.

Jack called in sick to work on the project, which instantly became his all-consuming passion. With Emmy's eager assent he established the goal of launching in one month. By mid-morning he had registered a domain name, by noon he'd hooked her up with a webmaster, and then he sequestered the seed money from their joint account. She promised to repay every penny, but he snapped his head. "What's mine is yours," he said, and withdrew like a knight from the presence of the queen.

She did not follow him to the bedroom and he didn't call for her, for make-up sex would cheapen the moment. Awash in soft silence, she sat herself down before the Mac in the dim light of a desktop lamp and set her fingers on the keyboard like a pianist. She threw her head back to receive an idea and attacked the keyboard, and filled page after page with ideas for *Tink!*. The first issue's theme: Keep Magic Alive. The overall theme: keeping the dream of a great life alive—a life of integrity, wonder, and love. Ten hours later she pushed away from the Mac, elated and exhausted, and changed into her cami in the silver bars of moonlight extruded by the shutters. She lifted the covers and laid down on her back, pressed her hip against his, squeezed the hand that he offered even in sleep. The whooshing of cars swept her away to a billowy land of joy.

Clap For Tink! launched ahead of schedule with a gauzy homepage in purples and pinks and a scalloped black margin embroidered with literary marginalia. There were fiction and poetry from a slew of old literary friends, and poetry from Jack himself, who was blocked until contemplation of his freezing night in King's Canyon inspired a flurry of lines about keeping the fire of wonder alive. "The Victorian Parlor" page hosted chats about Austen and the Brontë's and such, "The Schooner" hosted adventure tales, and the book review section was seeded by Emmy's own reviews of books that she read every night until three. The zine received four-hundred hits the first week, nine-hundred the second, and eleven-hundred the third. The submissions streamed in. "My people have come," Emmy said with a glow.

On a Saturday morning, with *Tink!* well underway, Jack lay on the sofa with eyes closed, trolling for taglines. But the focus and confidence he'd enjoyed before *Tink!* arrived had deserted him. So he abandoned the effort and gazed at Emmy, who sat purposefully straight composing personalized email rejection notes to writers, praising in each a nicely-turned phrase, an intriguing image, or the writer's good intentions, and exhorting each to "Keep Tink alive!" Jack gazed as if at a garden in bloom, then arose and kissed the nape of her neck, redolent of May berries. She didn't turn, but reached her hand back to clamp his hand to her shoulder. "Every story," she marveled, gazing at a submission on the screen, "hides human treasure beneath mounds of verbal and emotional debris. Fear. Insecurity. Love. Self-delusion. It's so naked and raw, you just want to embrace them and shield them from harm." She turned and smiled. "You want to exult at the sweet human concourse."

He nodded with appreciation for her compassion, then retreated to the couch and tried, but failed, to devise a tag line for *President Goufov*, a comedy about a Russian slacker accidentally elected President of the United States. He tried for a frustrating hour to focus, then something inside him broke loose at the roots.

At the office, Evyn scowled. "You're in boiling water, my hot little friend. You're missing deadlines right and left—and that's not the worst of it. For the love of all that is good, what is this *insane* trailer you wrote! Let me set the stage. It's the Cold War. A spy plane with an American pilot: Nebraska strong, handsome. An A-List action star! He's shot down over Russia, and captured by a sickle-wielding communist farmer who chains him to a tractor and runs to fetch the authorities. While he's away, the farmer's daughter—gorgeous, leggy, another A-Lister—falls in love with the pilot and frees him. They flee through the Caucasus—with the Red Army *and* the CIA in hot pursuit! We've got Action! Excitement! Adventure! And Sex! Lots! In other words, all the usual shit! And you give me ...?" Evyn set stylish glasses athwart a long narrow nose and peered down at Jack's text like a judge on high. "'Their love was bigger than two titanic nations with one common goal:' ... so far, so good ... 'to tear them apart' ... uh huh, standard fare ... '*for the sake of an American military-industrial complex needing heightened tensions to feed its lust for money and power, and a Soviet regime using fear to maintain its iron grip on its people.*'! I've got just one question for you: Are you insane!"

"*War* is."

"*War* is."

Jack nodded. "It's the military-industrial complex that's the real villain of this film, Evyn, because it needs war, or the constant threat of war, to justify our obscene military expenditures. It's the same with Iraq. I've got Eisenhower's farewell address right here in my briefcase, and that's just what he said."

"And *I've* got a file cabinet stuffed with the resumes of twenty bazillion English majors! So consider your answer to one simple question." Evyn peered across her glasses at Jack. Her gaze, even now, did not lack desire. "Is this *really* what you think our trailer should say?"

Jack did not have to think. "It's *exactly* what it should say."

She indicated the door with a flip of her fingers. And Poof! Jack was gone.

And Poof! *Clap For Tink!* was the tonic for Emmy. She worked on the zine for four or five tireless hours per day between waitressing shifts, reading pounds of submissions, writing kindly letters to submitters, editing stories with loving care, and promoting the zine in chat rooms, cafés, and a dozen more ways. Within half a year it was garnering 9,000 page views per month, by year's end 21,000—and when it was nominated for a Webby, Jack launched the "Webby For Emmy!" campaign. But Emmy's part-time waitressing and Jack's sporadic handyman work brought in little money; so Jack, with the delicacy of a man approaching a fairy on a leaf, posed practical suggestions for monetizing the zine. Ads. Subscriptions. Fees for click-through's to Amazon. But all were non-starters, for Emmy cherished her role as a guardian of fine literature, and feared the insidious power of money. He read all this in her wry fairy smile.

Inevitably, it was back to the Bay. Emmy went back to school for an English masters and a teaching credential, and kept *For Tink!* alive on a non-monetized basis while Jack made good bread as a carpenter's apprentice. When Emmy landed her first teaching job, *Clap For Tink!*

proudly showcased fiction and poetry by her open-hearted high school students. Her income now secure, Emmy tapped Jack on the head with her wand. "Hit the road, Jack," she said, and that's what he did. While she labored at home, he built homes in Georgia with Habitat For Humanity, taught English in Mali, spent four months visiting Indian locales from the stories of Kipling.

When he came home it was his turn for grad school. He emerged as Mr. Gardner, the passionate English teacher. He taught the high school canon with gusto, with extra ardor for his idols: Hemingway, Steinbeck, London. Mr. Gardner was loved for his love of literature, his masculine warmth, his good-humored patience, and the signature feature of his course, the hikes he led to literary locales throughout Northern California. Sometimes Ms. Gardner came along on the trips with kids from her school, and at suppertime the Gardners would scoop homemade campground chili into sourdough bowls. At campfire time Emmy would go off with the girls, mostly, to play Jane Austen *Mad Libs* and brainstorm story scenarios, while Jack would peel the boys off for campfire chats about life and literature—with the hidden agenda of delivering the subliminal message that if a masculine woodsman like Mr. Gardner liked literature, they could, too. Once, in the confessional darkness of a smoldering campfire at Jack London State Park, Jack revealed that the self-assured Mr. Gardner had once been bullied by mouth-breathers in high school for loving lit. This moved a spindly boy, whom Mr. Gardner had defended against hallway harassment arising from his love of poetry, to nickname Jack *Mr. Antolini* in honor of the *Catcher in the Rye* teacher who had covered the bloodied body of a sensitive boy bullied out the window to his death.

Jack and Emmy's tenth wedding anniversary fell at the end of the school year in June, and they embarked at once on a trip of Emmy's devising up the Pacific Coast to a distant destination she refused to divulge. Past the hillside dairy farms of western Marin they drove ... past the apple orchards of Sonoma ... through the great redwood forests of Humboldt ... along the bluffs and dunes of the Oregon coast ... through Washington back roads towns frozen in the '50s ... through British Columbia's massive fir forests ... and along the Klondike Highway through the Yukon. They camped in a secluded dell near a creek that they reasonably believed to be the creek followed by the doomed tenderfoot in "To Build A Fire." They hiked the creek seven miles up and seven back, and at night fell exhausted into each other's arms. The next morning, at sunrise, she laid him down in the center of a fairy ring of soft-purple fireweed, bright-white yarrow, smiling yellow arnica, and spired blue lupin—tall and waving, nodding at their joy.

The Petting Zoo

It's weird when you're eleven and run into your teacher at Walgreen's or Target. It's even weirder when you walk into your dad's apartment and find her in the bathroom in his old robe, like last week. "Oops! Sorry!" I pulled the door shut. Why? I don't know. She wasn't naked, just brushing her teeth. In my dad's robe. Her teeth are nice. I'm in love with her, frankly.

She opened the door. "Hello, Brandon." Her mouth was foamy. You could tell she brushed well. I guess she meant what she said about teeth. I hate teachers who tell you one thing and do another. She looked embarrassed, sucking the toothpaste back into her mouth. She was waiting for me to say hi, I guess. But I couldn't. Too dizzy. I didn't know if I should call her Ms. Landis. So I said I forgot something in my room, and then I forgot where my room was. Then I remembered and ran in there.

Dad knocked. "Hey, Sport." Sport. Ever since he moved out last summer, Dad's been trying nicknames on me. Sport. Dude. Trooper. Droogie. Like my regular name isn't good enough anymore. Like our regular life isn't. "Hey Sport. Wassup?"

Wassup. Puke. Wassup. "Nothin'."

"Hmm." Dad sat down on the bed next to me. I grabbed my phaser and started blasting droids. Zip-Zip! Zip-Zip! Zip-Zip! Zotz! Dad hates toy guns, but he ignored it because he knew I was freaked. "Hey Ace, remember I told you I'm friends with Ms. Landis?" Yeah, uh huh, sure. "Well guess what? She did a sleepover last night!"

Oh, she did a *sleepover!* Like I'm a fool. "Since when do grownups do sleepovers?" Jerk.

Dad put up his hands. "Put that gun down, Droogie." It wasn't a real gun, it was fake, which he knew.

"What the hell's a *droogie*, Dad?"

"Don't swear, Ace." Dad has that kind sort of face, with laugh lines around his eyes. The laugh lines are white but the rest of his face is red-ish, from being in the sun all the time. "I didn't expect you to get so upset, pal."

"Who's upset!"

"Aw, come on, kiddo." Dad stared at his fingernails. There was black dirt under them. His hands always have this great smoky smell of the planting mix he uses—organic mushroom mix, the best. Ms. Landis knocked, though the door was open. She was dressed. Faded jeans and a flowery blouse. Hardly any makeup. She looked great. I mean, *great*. She looks great in school, too, but that's a different kind of great, more official. This time, at Dad's, she looked more natural. Softer. "I think I'd better go," she told Dad. He got up and stood there looking at her, and they stood staring at each other for a long time like idiots, like there was that glass prison window between them. Then they started leaning towards each other like piles of bricks tipping over. "Goodbye! Adios! Sayonara!" I said. Dad took her hand and half shook it, half held it, like he couldn't decide. "I'll call you," he told her, and Ms. Landis said, "Bye, Brandon." I looked away and blasted some droids. Then I watched her walk out. She looks so nice walking. But I wasn't letting my dad off that easy. "I wanna talk to my mom!" I said. I called her "my mom" because she was *my mom*. *My* mom, not his. She was still in the car going home. I knew she missed me, she said so when she dropped me off. And she could still take me home.

"Come on now, Sport, let's talk this over." Dad looked worried. About Mom's lawyer, maybe.

"Is Ms. Landis coming back?"

"We'll talk about that later, Ace," which meant maybe. "It must be weird having a teacher in the house, huh, pal?"

"Duh, whatever." I shrugged Dad's hand off my shoulder and looked around my crummy room. It's half the size of my real room at home, and the window's cracked. I missed Bilbo. He lives with Mom. Lives with *me*, I mean. "You *do* still live with Dad, Brandon," Mom tells me. "*And* you live with me. Just not at the same time." So, yeah, I still live with my dog. 71% of the time.

"I know how you feel, Sport."

"What's for lunch?"

"Didn't you just have breakfast, Ace?"

What did *that* mean? I'll tell you what it meant, it meant he was worried about my weight. He's always worried about other people's weight, like Mom's weight, even though she's not fat. *Definitely* not. He's just stubborn. No matter how many times you tell him about her glands, he just smiles this know-it-all smile like he doesn't believe you. Once he said, "Frankly, son, it's her fork, not her glands." So I decided to stop wasting my breath. "Duh I had breakfast, I wouldn't be asking about *lunch* if I didn't."

Dad never gets too upset, he's a pretty chill guy. With us, it's party time all the time. "We'll make something good," he said, and I knew he would, he's such a great cook. Grilled cheese, fish sticks, hot dogs, you name it. "Nothing's too good for my partner," he says. "Here," he said, "punch me in the gut." His gut is hard because he earns his muscles from good, hard work. He's a landscape architect, so he digs all the time. The plates on his pickup say "I DIG." Cool. He always tells me to punch him in the gut, and I do but I always hold back. I don't wanna kill my only dad! I held back that time, too... *not.* "Oomph," Dad said. He sounded like the steam press at the cleaners Mom goes to. He threw me on the couch and got me in a headlock. I pounded his gut all rat-a-tat-tat!, and he acted like I shot him and fell forward, but he stepped on his rake and got a big bump on his forehead.

Mom and Dad got a friendly divorce, Mom's scary lawyer made sure of that. Mom bragged about her to her friends until the bills got obscene. I thought she was on Mom's side, but she just wanted money, frankly. Mom tells me not to listen when she talks about the divorce, but she's always talking about it right in front of me, so what's she expect? And it's interesting. Once Mom was on the phone with her lawyer, and she put her finger on her lip and said, "No, I don't *think* he's hiding any money," and, "Yes, I *know* he's a gardener." Okay, look: he's a *landscape architect*, why the hell can't she get that? Then I started thinking, is Dad hiding money in the holes he digs? Then I thought, no, that would be dumb, his customers could lie and say it's theirs. Mom's lawyer always harassed Dad on the phone, and he had to waste money he needed to pay child support for me to hire his own stupid lawyer to call Mom's stupid lawyer so she wouldn't waste our quality time. "No need to expose you to this crap," he told me.

Mondays are weird. I have fun with Dad all weekend, then Mom picks me up from school, and *whoosh*—soccer, homework, bedtime, stress. "*Some*one has to be the grown-up," Mom says. I'm still just eleven, that's an extreme duh. I feel rotten on Mondays. Really rotten last Monday. "Rainy days and Mondays always get you down," she sang, some old song. My stomach hurt big time. "No wonder," she said, "with that gunk Dad feeds you."

We eat good food at Mom's, but it's different than the good food at Dad's. Mom's food is like magazine food, with bright colors and all the major food groups. Dad's food is pale, all yellow and white. If I pick at Mom's food, she stares at me like I'm dying, like she feels guilty. So I start packing it away, and then she looks at me like I'm the *American Idol* winner. We watch that together.

"Dad's got a new friend," I said last Monday, because I was bored.

"Oh?" Mom spends hours pulling hairs out of her eyebrows to make them look thin. She raised one eyebrow and it looked like a question mark.

"Yep," I said, "Ms. Landis."

"Oh *really?*" Her eyebrow climbed higher. Dad told her she couldn't do that if she bought Botox, a big ripoff, so I guess she didn't.

"Yeah," I said. I was packing it away. Mom makes veggies taste great, and her regular stuff, like meat loaf and lasagna, is über good too. It's like truth serum on me. And that eyebrow is scary. "They had a sleepover," I said.

She screeched like a cat. "Really?"

"Yeah, really. Jesus, Mom, grownups have sleepovers like kids do."

Her eyebrow sunk, her whole body sunk and she picked up her real estate magazine and hid her face behind it while I ate. Then she got on the phone while I cleared the dishes. "Don't listen," she told me. Okay! I'm deaf! Her friends told her to pay The Dark Sorceress to change the custody thing, and also call the school to get that little b-word fired (they actually *said* the b-word), and she should sleep with Dad's bestie, Ron, for revenge, 'cause everyone knows he's hot for her. "La la la! La la la!" I was seriously trying *not* to hear now. Bilbo started howling right along with me. "Okay, I'm deaf!" But I heard enough on her end of the phone.

"Brandon, *please*. I'm trying to talk!" Jesus, lady, what did I do? Into my room, merrily merrily merrily.

The first day at school after I saw her in Dad's bathroom, Ms. Landis had her school face on. I walked past her desk and smiled this weird smile, but she pretended not to see me. She had her great smell, patchouli. Dad told me man to man that he likes hippie chicks. It was cool that I recognized her smell from Dad's bathroom, like she belonged to me sort of. She asked if any of us saw any good movies last weekend. Our hands all shot up. She called on Justin. Tanisha. Consuela. Tucker. Kimberly. Eduardo. Valentina. Hello! I'm waiting! My arm was getting tired. I raised it to the ceiling like I had to pee, but she still didn't see me. I kept waving my arm. *Finally* she called me. I was gonna tell her about this war flick *Casablanca* Dad rented, but I decided to talk about *The Parent Trap* instead.

"*The Parent Trap*, Brandon?" She looked nervous. She knew.

"Yeah. It's this great flick about these twins whose parents get divorced. The parents really love each other still, but they can't stop fighting. So each parent gets one of the twins, and they grow up apart. Then the parents meet up again a lot of years later, and the twins get together and make the parents see how dumb they were to break up in the first place. But some messed-up lady tries to ruin everything by marrying the dad, even though no one wants her there." Ooo, direct hit. She said "I see" in this dying little voice and ran out of the room.

Saturday morning it was back to Dad's. I hate going there. Not the being with Dad, but looking at myself with my stupid plastic trash bags in the tacky mirrors in the elevator, then walking down the hall with its stupid yellow vomity carpet, with dumb kids looking at me like "Who are *you*?" even though I live there 29% of the time. Dad's door was unlocked, like always. Mom's door has two locks and a chain, and she uses them all the time since Dad left. Frankly, they're incompatible, though they were compatible enough to have me, duh. I walked in with my phaser out.

"Hey there, dude!" Dad had shaving cream on his face and a towel on. His smile drooped when he saw me aiming at him. "You can put your gun down. She's not here." He's not totally as dumb as he looks.

"Oh yeah?" I said. "That's too bad." Dad looked at me like he didn't believe me, then he finished shaving, then he made bagels and put them on this little metal table we found on the sidewalk. I slopped cream cheese on one. "What are we gonna do today?" I asked him.

"Oh, I thought we'd do something a little different," he said. But first we played X-Box, and then we went down to wash the truck. Dad put the tailgate down and I climbed into the bed, and he handed me the hose with the high-powered nozzle. I blasted the leaves and grass out the back of the truck. Then he put the game on and we listened while we soaped up the truck. He flicked some soapy water at me and I got him back big time, twice as bad as he got me. Then we rinsed the truck and dried it, and we hardly even talked except for "hand me a towel" or "fill the bucket" and stuff. Dad likes silence, but Mom hates it. She's The Chatterbox, and he's The Mute. Dad gave the truck a big thumbs up. "Hey Droog, I thought we'd go to the zoo today. Your mom's gonna be there."

"She is?"

"Your mom and I thought, hey, just because we're not married anymore doesn't mean we can't spend time with our favorite guy, right?"

Yeah I guess. Sure.

Mom met us inside where the peacocks walk around. She was wearing the pantsuit she wears when she tries to sell houses. *Tries* to sell houses. Hi, Susan. Hello Rob. Did you have trouble parking? Why? You're the one who's late. "*Funny!*" I said. I just meant it's crowded. I found a good space. Well, good. Did he eat? Of course, he ate like a champ. "Hey guys, come on! The animals are waiting." I walked in between them like I used to. "Hey, look," I said, "there's a jaguar! Hey look, you guys, that bird sleeps standing up!" Dad's jaw was tight, like when this idiot customer complained that the sprinkler Dad put in threw the water too far onto the sidewalk (like, a half an inch or something psycho like that). Mom was a little more interested in the animals than Dad. She said, Oh look, Brandon, I never knew giraffes had such long tongues. Yep, Dad said, they do. He was getting into it now. He said, Look, Brandon, penguins. I'm glad *I* don't have to dress for work like that. "Good one, Dad!" Mom's lips made a sour lemon pucker, but I made a clown face and made her laugh. We kept walking, Dad on my right and Mom on my left. Gorillas are smart, aren't they son? Hey, look at that chimp. Hey, look at those gorillas. Hey, look at that lemur. The talk started to slow down like a battery dying. Hey lookit that possum. That anteater. Hippo. Hey lookit those zebras. That rhino. Those penguins. Those *penguins?* Christ Almighty, we've been here already. So what? So you should've gotten a map like I said. We don't need a *map.* Oh really? Yes, really. I suppose we're not lost? How could we be *lost,* it's the freaking zoo, not the damn Amazon. There's no need for sarcasm and curses. I wanted cotton candy. I didn't know who to ask, because I didn't want them to fight about it. So I asked Dad if I could have cotton candy, but I looked at Mom so she'd think I was asking her too. She said, "I don't mind if your dad doesn't mind." "I don't *mind,* I'm just broke." "Oh, you're broke." So she gave me a fiver and made a dumb snort.

Other kids were running to the food stand. I wanted to run but my legs got wobbly, so I just kept walking next to Mom and Dad, slow. It was like earlier in the day, in the petting zoo. We used to go there when I was small, and we'd pose for pictures. I know it sounds dumb, but I wanted to do it again just for fun. So I was petting this calf, and the zookeeper told us about this awful thing they do to make veal. What they do is, they keep the calves in these tiny little pens so they can't even move. Their muscles don't grow because they don't get any exercise, and they get so weak they can't even walk. It felt that way.

Donuts

Be home at six, it's the same every day: *Donnie, dear, you be home at six. Are you listening, Donnie?!"* News flash, Mom, it's *stupid* to be home at six, I can ride down the hill maybe ten more times before it gets dark. *How many times do I have to explain this, son—dinner is our special time. Our time to be together, son.* Sure it is, Mom—we stare at our plates and I get another dumb lecture about slacking, and then I get to hear about my perfect little brother. So if Dougie's so great, why'd Dad disappear? *God* she's dumb. Whoa, check the sky out over the ocean—all red and orange like that tank explosion in *Medal of Valor*! Road's clear down below... two block shot... *Whoosh!* Doing sixty! *Man* what a bike, love the wind on my face, like it's slapping my face, wet and salty—I *love* it!

***

God-damn grinding gears, if that's the transmission I'm screwed with the clutch, and the brakes shrieking like Tina on the phone, and the credit card maxed out at three-thou already. Five-thousand debt after *six years* painting houses while *she* coasts at home, and now *she* gets the—oops! We interrupt this rant for a recorded message from your newly ex-wife: *This may be a little hard for you to understand, Robert, but taking care of our home and your daughter is hard work, too—in fact, I may work even harder than you. At least* you *get to be out in the fresh air all day*! Ha ha! Good joke! I got it, Teen, even with my limited education! We return you now to our regular rant: *Six years* hard labor while she coasts at home, and now *she* gets the good car, and *I* get the shaft! The *crank*shaft, that's a good one! I'm gonna *do* it, god damn it, I'm gonna do stand-up like everyone says! And she can't tell me not to, I'm a free man now, free, I can do what I want to... *except* spend my money, and see my own daughter whenever I want. Hey, that's *more* good material, no wonder comedians have messed up lives. Hey, where's the recorder... right here on the seat. You're *so good*, Bobby, you can drive with one hand, work the mike with the other—like in middle school, working the Walkman while biking... and in high school, spinning the best donuts. Man, I'd love to see her face in the crowd when I'm a stand-up star, killing them with my ex-wife jokes. Sweet!

***

Yo Fooj, check this donut! This bike's *awesome*, dude, go stand down there, I'll spin it next to you. Watch, you gotta go fast to really stick it. *Whoosh!* Goin' eighty downhill, *at least*! Wind's good! Grind it now, Donnie, stick it! *Whew*! *Major rubber*! Hey Fooj, where we goin'? To the park? Whatchya got there, a cigarette, man? Hey dude, that's a joint. Ooo, that smells nasty. *Duh*, I've smelled grass! *No* I ain't scared, how stupid is that! *No* I wouldn't get a whacking, my dad's not like that. What's he like? Shut up, Fuji, I'm going back biking.

***

Jee-zus, will you look at this crap? Half the houses need paint jobs, and the ones that have been painted were painted by homeowners too cheap to pay a pro. How the hell is a working man supposed to carry two apartments and a wife who says eighty-five dollar salon visits are *a business necessity, Robert, if I'm going to get a decent admin assistant job*. Nine frickin' hours without a break, better stop at The Mast for a burger and brew—hell, I can't pick up Jen until seven anyway, *You're not allowed to pick her up before seven, Robert, you can read the court order as well as I can*. Damned if I'm gonna get there early and sit in front of her highness's building like a dog while Jen looks out the window at her dad, waiting for his *vis-i-ta-tion* to start.

***

Cheese-us, Fuji is *so* frickin' stupid! Dad's so cool, he used to race motorbikes downhill like this! Didn't he? *Yeah,* he did, I'm *sure* that he did, Mom's crazy when she says I'm too young to remember, his hair long and blond like mine, flying behind him like mine, I'm *glad* I've got cool hair like him—I'm a *playah*, dude, those Chinese girls *love* me! That tall girl wants to go to the movies. *Whoa,* my god! Look at that dork with the bike helmet on! Dad would *never* make me wear one, he never did. Mom's so dumb: *You need to wear your helmet, Donnie, I spent twenty-eight dollars I can't afford to protect that everlovin' noggin of yours!* Sure, Mom, that'll happen. Whoosh! Ha! That dork's staring at me with his mouth open. In his dreams he can go this fast, I shot that block in about *ten seconds!* Man, I gotta get home soon. Aw, forget it, what's Mom gonna do, cry?

***

Hey Tom, here's my latest. How many feminist divorce lawyers does it take to screw in a lightbulb? Answer? None. They don't screw in lightbulbs, they only screw fathers! Hey Tommy, you smiled! You *smiled,* bartender, don't deny it! I know, I know, you're supposed to be neutral—but face it, Tommy, there's just us guys here, and you smiled, you did. Which means you're *hooked.* See, I hooked you with my lead, 'cause that's what you do—you hook them with your lead, then you get rolling on your theme and all. Like: You know why they call a woman's butt *booty?* 'Cause they wreck your marriage, they *boot* you out, then they get a butch lawyer and take all the booty! And how is that possible? How can that be? Because this is the land of *no-fault* divorce. *No fault,* Tommy, like World War II—a *no-fault* war! Like, "Hey, Germany! I guess our countries had *irreconcilable differences!* Hey, that's cool, let bygones be bygones. I'll give your country a boatload of support money, I'll visit the refugees two times a week, and before you know it, we'll be best friends!" And that, my beer-pouring friend, is history.

***

Man, I bet I've got the strongest legs in school from walking up this hill every day—and biking. I'm totally the coolest one. I mean check it out, what's Mom always ragging on Dougie about? *You know, Dougie, it's great to be an A student—and believe me, son, not a day goes by that I don't thank heaven for what you've done in school—but it's important to get some exercise, too.* Well look at *me*, Mom, that's *all* that I do! But with *me* it's always, *Why aren't you ever home on time! Can't you ever think of anyone besides yourself?* How much sense does *that* make! Whoa dude, I'm *flying*!

***

Hey God, are you listening? I know you're up there, I can hear you laughing—even over my dying transmission! So listen, God, with you as my witness—because you *were there* in the bar with me, right? *Duh* you're *every*where, cha!—all I had was *one glass*, right? You know it, and I know it, and every breathalyzer out there knows it. But you *also* know that if our dear little Tina—who you put on Earth to torment me, Big Dawg—smells beer on my breath, she'll sick her lawyer on me like a junkyard dog. Which is why you, in your infinite wisdom, made breath spray for poor slobs like me. Which is ... where? On the seat, like everything else. Everything I *own*, practically. Look at these yups driving home in their Audis. What the hell do they do downtown all day? Whatever it is, Tina thinks it's just great. 'Cause that's what she wants, a rich guy with clean hands. Man, the days are getting short fast. Poor little kids—first vacation ends, then the days get short. Party's over, little buds.

***

Flying downhill with the air so cold, it feels like being whipped by the wind! I bet it feels like this when you're skiing, I am *totally* going skiing one day! I'll ski all day, then go inside for hot chocolate and—*whoa*, tonight's soup! What kind did Mom say? *Tomato rice*! She's gonna cry, *I made your favorite and you couldn't even be home on time*! I'm coming, Mama! I'm just your sweet everlovin' little rascal, that's all!

***

Wait a minute, seven-thirty or seven? Jen would laugh if she saw me stroke my beard: *Dad, you look like you're trying to look smart when you play with your goat!* That's *goatee*, hon. Damn, seven-twenty! If it's seven I'm screwed, she won't let me see Jennie at all: *It's not good for the child to sit there waiting for her father to arrive, Robert, can you imagine how it feels when you don't show up?* Oh shut the hell up, *one time* I forget and I'm marked for life! Where's that court order! Right—

***

One last dip, and I *glide* to the driveway!

***

What the—

***

Pickup!

***

Slam it! Donut!

***

Nail it, Donnie! Stick it! Donut!

***

Braaakes!

Kool Brother Rat

How cool, at thirteen, was my cool big brother, dubbed *Kool King Rat* by his cool-kid friends for his lucrative business selling Kool cigarettes behind the boys' bathroom a la shrewd King Rat of the prison camp film? So cool that when he and his friends played department store ditch in the May Company, my bro had the brass to hide in a pallet of pillows in the basement loading dock in the off-limits bowels of the store before being nabbed by a six-foot-four security guard with a handlebar 'stache and an Eastwood sneer who said these words as he kicked my bro out with a boot to the butt: "If you ever set foot in my shop again, I'll kick your sweet ass back to Kalamazoo!" This was L.A., and no one knew where Kalamazoo *was*— but "I'll kick your sweet ass back to Kalamazoo!" became *the* catch-phrase for my cool big bro and his friends that year.

How undeniably cool was my bro at thirteen? So cool that he personally invented rooftop mountaineering, the object of which was to climb up onto Jerry Weinberg's house at one end of the block and cross all the way to the Bartletts' house at the other end without once setting foot on the ground. To do this you had to step or jump from rooftop to rooftop, or swing yourself across by a tree branch. Legend had it that my brother and Eddie Elsbree had spied Mr. Krieger, the eighth-grade math teacher, smoking grass in his yard while listening to Dylan.

How supremely cool was my bro at thirteen? So cool that he rigged a triple spy-mirror system which allowed him to look out our bedroom door, down the hall, and into our parents' room to watch *The Tonight Show* long after bedtime. He'd made a rudimentary listening device with an amplifier and a lamp shade, and was able to enjoy three months' worth of Johnny Carson's monologues until Dad discovered the mirrors while he shimmied in his heart-covered boxers for Mom.

How cool, in contrast, *wasn't I* at thirteen? I was so uncool that I had earned an *Excellent* in citizenship in every grade from first through seventh, and was recklessly heading for the honor roll with a month left in eighth grade. I was so uncool that when my mom complained to our next-door neighbor over coffee that kids these days were so out of control she had sprouted some premature gray, she patted my head and added, "I don't mean *you* of course, honey," as I held the sugar bowl like a proper English butler. I was so uncool that when a bunch of us went to a birthday sleepover at the apartment of Rick De Leon, the undisputed hellion king of our old elementary school, I was one of the kids too scared to follow Rick down into the excavated construction site at the corner after midnight, and had to spend half the night listening to Rick and Marcus Burgess talking about how cool—*Cool!*—it had been to climb up onto the steam shovel in the dark of night. How cool, in short, was I *not* at thirteen? So painfully uncool that I would have tried anything, with childhood fading, to claim my birthright as a red-blooded, hell-raising, All-American bad boy in the storied tradition of my cool big brother and his cigarette-sneaking, Playboy-peeking, shoplifting, rock-throwing, trespassing friends.

But first I needed a partner in crime. The logical choice was my best friend, Morty, who always had been my right-hand man. When I started a humor magazine in the mold of *Mad* in sixth grade, Morty created a teacher-baiting cartoon character named RatPuss who used mind control to make the principal's hair fall out—we got detention when a copy found its way to our bald principal. And when I launched an *I Hate The Brady Bunch* anti-fan club at the start of eighth grade, it was Morty who put together an ironic party featuring Monkees records, Cheese Whiz on Wonder Bread, Jell-O, and a mandatory dress code of bell bottoms and vests. The party—ironically—only harmed my stunted rep for coolness when two girls who didn't get the joke spread tales at school of my "really neat" Brady Bunch party. Nevertheless, Morty was my man.

"But *why?*" Morty asked, peering through black horned rims as I explained rooftop mountaineering. "I don't get it."

"What's to *get*, man?

"The *angle*, Steiny, the ironic perspective. What are you *after*? A subversive glimpse into the banal private lives of the middle class? Something Warholesque?" Morty was getting *way* too excited. He was rubbing his palms together just as he had when he got the idea of us running laps in P.E. shackled at the ankles; the irony was lost on our Neanderthal gym coach, who took an instant and enduring dislike to the two of us which meant nothing to Morty but meant something to me, since it cost me any shot at playing in the Mission Bell football game. "Maybe we should take pictures of the yards from the rooftops, all those manicured little yards with their identical green lawns, and make a collage! Or drop Campbell's soup cans into the yards!"

"You don't get this, Morty! There's nothing ironic about it. It's just good old-fashioned American boy stuff. Huck Finn stuff!"

Morty squinted. "*Huck Finn boy stuff?*" He really was trying to understand.

"Yes, Morty. Jeez, it's a rite of passage. We're *supposed* to do this."

"Like Huck Finn, you mean?"

"Exactly! C'mon, it'll grow hair on your chest." I wasn't thinking of chest hair, however, but the precocious goatee Kool King Rat had grown at thirteen.

Morty cocked his head and grinned. The idea evidently struck him as so far over the top that it went beyond irony into a whole new realm of cool. "Alright! I'll do it! I'll do Huck Finn boy stuff!" So we started down the block towards Jerry Weinberg's house. My brother was across the street, shooting the breeze with Ollie Wirtz and a couple of other guys who were working under the hood of Ollie's Camaro. He was looking our way, but Morty and I were as invisible to him as we had been forever. Fine. Further down the block, Mrs. Rosen, whose pretty face and soft curves had begun to stir something wiggly in me of late, was looking for her lost cat in the bushes. Across the street, Susie Margolis was making drip candles in the shade of her front porch. Did I say *Susie*? I mean, *Susie!* The angel-faced brainiac whom we had all sensed throughout elementary school was years ahead of us in knowledge and wisdom, and whose Mona Lisa smile assured us that we shouldn't worry so much about our future in the adult world, because she had seen it, and it wasn't that bad. Susie—*mon cherie amour*! —whose long brown hair and oversized wire-frames made her look like a little Gloria Steinem (who, my brother once told me in a conspiratorial whisper at the dinner table, was not just a big women's libber, but a *genuine former Playboy bunny*!). Yes, Susie! Who had walked the block for McGovern, made her own tie-dyed shirts, and, most important of all, had given me hope for everlasting happiness by saying recently, "Maybe you're not such a Neanderthal after all, Steinmetz," after looking at my black-magic peace sign during art class (she didn't know it was the Mercedes emblem). Ah, Susie. If she knew of the daring exploits I was about to attempt—well, like all girls she was a mystery to me, but I guess I thought she'd think I was cool.

We looked around as we reached the corner, then crept into the alley behind Jerry Weinberg's house. The back fence had a three-foot-high masonry bottom topped by corrugated plastic in a wood frame. Morty hummed the *Mission Impossible* theme and we both cracked up. Then we climbed to the top of the fence where it abutted the garage. From there we were able to reach our arms up over a corner of the garage and hoist ourselves up with a hop, though it took every ounce of Gumby-armed Morty's strength to do it. "You made it!" I told him. Morty made an elaborate comic commando pantomime to indicate our next move, but his wild hippie hair, thick glasses, and deadpan expression just made me laugh harder. "Stainers!" I cried as I looked around the roof. Stainers were a purplish-reddish hard berry great for staining surfaces. And dozens had fallen onto Jerry's garage. I gathered a handful, crept to the edge of the garage and took aim at Jerry's room. Pow! Pow! Pow! Pow! The white walls were decorated with dozens of purplish starbursts.

"It's like a tie-dyed house," Morty marveled.

"Or that psychedelic poster on my brother's wall."

The next house over belonged to Mr. Kleinfeld, an infamous grouch with a grudge against our family. He never gave candy on Halloween, and my big brother had fixed him one year with textbook execution of the ol' flaming-paper-bag-full-of-dog-crap trick. So I had to get onto the addition to the house and off again quick. The problem was, there was a several-foot gap between the Weinberg's garage and the Kleinfeld's addition.

"Looks like Snake River Canyon," Morty murmured down at the concrete ten feet below. We sized up the jump. With a running start, if we planted our feet on the adobe tile edging the Weinbergs' garage, we should be able to make the jump with a foot to spare. I was scared, I admit—and that gave me a thrill as I charged the edge of the garage and leaped into the air. I cleared the edge by half a foot, landed in a heap and looked back at Morty a mile away. Morty measured the jump and took three long strides without hesitation, launching himself from the edge of the garage with one arm stretched out like Fred Astaire leaping (Morty had, in fact, taken ballroom dance, and this had given him grace as well as something less desirable—just cause to be punched in the belly by an eighth-grade bully). Morty seemed weightless as he hung in the air like Dr. J; he looked as if he might float up into the sky like Peter Pan (though his thick black-framed glasses evoked the nightshirted John). As he sailed through the air— weightless, it seemed—a smile stretched Morty's lips, and his long hippie hair flapped in the breeze like Dumbo's ears. When he came down at last, he spread his arms like a ski jumper landing and bowed with a flourish. "Let's push on, Batman." I gaped at my friend.

The gap between the Kleinfeld addition and the Rosens' garage was too broad to leap; but I knew from my big brother's bedtime lore that a conveniently situated jacaranda tree spanned the gap. I grabbed a friendly branch overhanging the Kleinfelds' addition and swung onto a bough situated just above the Rosens' garage, but it snapped, and I tumbled onto the garage—along with a cat that fell into my lap with a shriek.

"You found Pepper!" cried Mrs. Rosen, looking up from down below.

I did? "Yes I did, Mrs. Rosen! I found your cat!"

Mrs. Rosen looked more stirring than ever in her soft white

sleeveless sweater, green eyes glowing with joy. She leaned a ladder against the garage, and I clambered down with her scared little kitty. "What did *big bad kitty* do to you?" purred Mrs. Rosen as I handed Pepper down. Some big bad kitty had evidently taken a bite out of Pepper's flank, and Pepper had taken refuge in the tree. "I don't know how to repay you," Mrs. Rosen told me. I was just thirteen and wasn't quite sure, but I had some ideas. The thudding answer came that night, when Mrs. Rosen bore a batch of homemade brownies to our door.

"Your little man's quite the hero," she told Mom.

"Another gold star for Mr. Good Boy," sneered my eleven-year-old sister.

I glanced at my brother, fearing he'd heard, and dreading the roll of disappointed eyes that would confirm my lingering lack of cool; but fortunately, the man was just reading—*Playboy*, most likely, hidden behind his chem book. The brownies were yummy, and my unexpected proximity to the lilac-scented Mrs. Rosen was intoxicating, but my expedition had failed: I had set out to be a rogue akin to a cat burglar, but had become a cat-saver. I needed to be bold to prove I was no Boy Scout—to earn my merit badge in bad-boy behavior.

So I talked Morty out of a trip to Hollywood to buy the new *Fantastic Four* and talked him into a trip to the neighborhood coffee shop to duplicate some of the restaurant pranks my big brother had told me about in late-night bull sessions. The first, a mere warm-up, was a gag on the waitress. The coffee shop featured a huge breakfast special: two eggs, hashed browns, three sausages, toast and juice for a buck-sixty-nine. When the waitress, a wax-faced gum-cracker named Betty, asked, "What'll it be?" I, like my brother before me, said: "Two breakfast specials, please."

She didn't even raise a pencil-thin brow, but jotted my order and turned to Morty. "How 'bout you, hon?"

This was all wrong. She was supposed to turn to go, having received the order for two breakfasts, and then Morty was supposed to call her back and say, "Excuse me, miss. *I'll* have two breakfast specials, too." And the poor fool was supposed to be shocked. Clearly she hadn't heard. "Excuse me, miss. I said I'll have two breakfast specials."

"And I heard you. Two breakfast specials." Again to Morty, "What's yours, sunshine?"

"I'll just have some toast, please," said Morty, and off she went.

"Great joke," said Morty, rolling his eyes.

"Forget it," I said. "Let's get on with the next."

Checking that no eyes were upon us, we eased ourselves into some empty booths nearby and *adjusted* things. I sat back down in front of the two huge plates of food I had ordered, and Morty stared at his toast. Making sure the waitress wasn't looking, I slid one of the plates across the table to Morty and bowed my head to eat, but heard a sweet familiar voice. "*You* may be due for another upward classification, Steinmetz," said Susie Margolis. "Your comment about *The Old Man and the Sea* yesterday was surprisingly perceptive."

It was? I knew I had made some wisecrack in English that had fallen flat, and that the teacher, deluded by the desire to see an eighth-grade boy take literature seriously, had misinterpreted it as a profundity; but I was shocked that Susie had done the same.

"Yes," said Susie, sizing me up with a gaze that could either lift me or shred me, "you definitely need to be reclassified as a Cro-Magnon, Steinmetz—with full Modern Man status, oh, a year away, maybe."

"Cool," I said, extruding scrambled egg. I stared up at the beneficently smiling Susie and then glanced at her folks, who both wore wire-framed glasses like Susie, and smiled the same knowing smile as she.

"What kind of goddess do you have to be," I asked Morty as Susie and her parents seated themselves, "to stop and talk to kids *with your parents right there?*"

"It *is* a wonder," said Morty. We stared at Susie as she chatted with her parents, who listened intently and nodded their heads—as if she were their equal. "Her dad's an English teacher," said Morty, as if that might explain Susie's unnatural comfort level with her folks. "And her mom plays classical piano."

"She's an only child," I mused. "Maybe they feel sorry for her, like they've *got* to listen to her." We studied Susie further. She said something with a grin, and her father threw his head back and laughed. *Man* was he putting an act on for her! Then the big moment came, he took the salt shaker. The cap, which I had loosened earlier, fell off as planned, and all the salt poured onto his eggs. Unfortunately, that idiot Morty gave out a shriek, and Susie swiveled her head and caught us watching with wide-open mouths. We knew Susie wouldn't rat us out—she was a kid, after all—but on her way out she stopped by our booth and traced a little circle on my scrambled eggs with a mouth-moistened finger, saying with the cool of a movie-star: "On second thought, Steinmetz, I think you're just a Homo Erectus... at best." Morty raised his head like a turtle peeking out of its shell: he liked Susie a lot, and clearly felt embarrassed. Susie frowned at him. "Et tu, Mor-tay?" she said, and Morty's head sank beneath her judgment. Susie raised her head up like a proud pony and led her parents out the door.

One more egg laid on the road to true cool. So like Kool King Rat of a few years before, I slunk behind the thick bushes at the back of our yard to stimulate my thoughts with tobacco—my first cigarette; my first puff of Dad's Kools. And my first volcanic cough, which raised a startled gasp from the secluded nook on the other side of the bushes. It was a girl who had been in the arms of my brother, who gave me a stern Look Of God as the girl straightened her sweater. Lesson learned: cigarettes are the pits. "I'm goin'a Morty's," I muttered as the girl settled back into my brother's arms.

Mrs. Rosen hailed me as I walked past her house. "Oh, Bobby! I heard you won an award at school!" Ollie Wirtz, who had stood lookout years before while Kool King Rat sold smokes in the schoolyard, looked up from under the hood of his Camaro. I smiled blankly at Mrs. Rosen as if I hadn't heard. "What did you win, Bobby?" she trilled. I shrugged and hustled along. "Wha'd you win, kid?" Ollie said with a cruel gleam. I ignored him too and walked faster—though not so fast as to look uncool. "The Best Essay award!" yelled Mr. Krieger, the math teacher, watering his lawn. I hastened my pace, coolness be damned. "*And* the Good Citizenship Medal!" added Mr. Krieger, may he rot in hell. My cheeks flushed at Ollie's obnoxious chortle.

"Morty," I pleaded, "it's time to get real," and told him about my latest brainstorm.

His negativity was a kick to the gut. "But I don't *want* to go shoplifting," he said, removing my grip from his scarecow arm.

"Why not!"

"I don't know, Steiny. It's just too non-ironic, I guess." I peered into his eyes. "And I guess I'm just tired of Huck Finn boy stuff."

"Only the roof climbing was Huck Finn stuff, Morty!" I said, and tried to explain how the restaurant pranks were something else entirely, and shoplifting was a whole new realm of excitement that we owed it to ourselves to try. "You've gotta get beyond categories, Morty. Forget whether it's *Huck Finn stuff*, or Marvel Comics stuff, or whatever—just do it because you've *gotta* do it, because it's your destiny to do it."

But Morty was in his stubborn mood, and it's no use reasoning with Morty in his stubborn mood. So he rode off on his Sting Ray, and I raced off on mine to Mike De Leon's apartment.

Mike's mom, a weathered Southern belle worn down by trying to control Mike, greeted me at the door as if I were royalty. She lived alone with Mike, and considered me a good influence on him. "Oh, *Mi*-key!" she trilled. "It's Bobby *Stein*-metz!" All the curtains in the living room were drawn, and the only light came from *Divorce Court* on the TV.

Mike stepped into the room like a prisoner summoned by the warden and stood with his hands crossed before him. "Hi," he said—not actually *say*ing "hi," but slowly raising one eyebrow, his most enthusiastic greeting.

"Hi," I replied the conventional way. Mike raised one side of his mouth in an Elvis sneer. He never raised both eyebrows at once, or both sides of his mouth at once to smile. There was always something off-center about him, some suggestion that he, like Susie, knew things beyond his years—but in the case of Mike, they were things I wouldn't want to know. "Want to go do stuff?" I asked.

He thought about it for a moment, pursed his lips and nodded. Mrs. De Leon had been standing between us with hands clasped, anxiously following our exchange—and the uncertainty of our plan alarmed her. "Do *what* stuff, Bobby! What stuff?"

"Just ride our bikes," I shrugged, and glanced at Mike, who nodded to indicate I'd done well.

"Will you be needing any milk from the store, Mother?" Mike asked. His mom always said she was raising Mike to be a proper Southern gentleman, but she wasn't buying an ounce of that crap.

"Just be home by supper," she said tartly. She fastened the top three buttons of Mike's shirt while whispering something hot into his ear, and she tugged the ear, hard, making Mike wince.

"What's up?" Mike asked as we raced our bikes down the street.

"I wanna go shoplifting," I said.

"Whoa," said Mike, skidding to a stop. "*You* wanna lift?" Mike and I had been casual friends for a few years because we both liked wild stuff like tackle football and bike racing, but there was a gulf between us because I never went along with his most wild schemes.

"Yeah," I said.

Mike's gray eyes gleamed. "Well *alright*, Steinmetz! Follow me."

We rode our bikes to Pico Boulevard and parked them around the corner from the Dime Store, where I'd been buying baseball cards for years. "No need to pay today," I joked.

"You're right about that, Steiny boy," said Mike. There was a back door opening onto the parking lot and a register near it. Since it was a Sunday, a mob of kids were buying candy and comics. Mike and I entered separately and stood on opposite sides of the mob, per his plan. Mike had said he'd start a diversion, but I was so shocked when he shoved a skinny kid that I just stood there gaping while the woman behind the register watched events unfold.

The shoved kid said "Hey," with some trepidation, and Mike said, "Sorry man, accident," and started brushing off the kid's shirt while shooting me a look to remind me to do my job—he was a natural-born leader. So I found my nerve and grabbed a handful of packs of baseball cards and dropped my hand to my side and walked out, and I kept walking, without looking back, until I reached our bikes around the corner, and raced to the 76 Station two blocks down. Mike met me at the dumpster a few minutes later.

"*Man*, that was cool!" I said, my heart still pounding.

Mike shook his head pitifully. I think, looking back, that he *agreed* it was cool, but felt it was against his code to say so—or maybe shoplifting had just became a job to him. Whatever the reason, he just said: "Wha'd you get?" I showed him the five packs of cards I'd swiped, and prepared to open them. But Mike grabbed my arm. "Don't," he said. "We'll sell 'em and split the money."

Sell 'em? Selling baseball cards was a concept I'd never heard of. Baseball cards were for gazing at, for organizing into albums, for loving—but selling? Never. "What do you want to do now?" I sighed.

"Let's go over to the school. There's something there that'll blow your mind."

John Burroughs Junior High was, in a limited sense, the most well-known school in the country because its brick façade was constantly used to establish a school setting in TV shows and movies. I followed Mike to the side of the school. We hid our bikes behind some bushes and edged along the side of the building behind the bushes. "You can't tell anybody," Mike said, and I knew I'd better not. Mike removed a loose grill from the wall that vented the crawl space beneath the school and climbed feet-first halfway into the opening, signaling me to follow. I lowered myself after him and—*whoa*. In the glow of a couple dozen candles, sitting on crates playing cards, were a rogue's gallery of some of the biggest troublemakers in school. There were Rafi and Dirk Nimsky, oldest of the four Nimsky brothers, unibrow blockheaded bullies who were two years apart in age and looked like an evil version of Russian nesting dolls when they lined up against the chain-link fence in the playground shaking kids down for pocket change; Marcus Burgess, a hyper blond scarecrow who always got F's and was constantly suspended for reasons unknown; and Richard Horowitz, who bragged about torturing cats with pen knives.

"*Whoa*," I said. "What is this, Club Fire Trap?" I was trying to warn them in a humorous way that they could burn the school down with all those candles set loosely in melted wax. Their expressions ranged from hostile to blank, and Mike assured them: "He's cool. We were just lifting at the Dime Store. Show 'em what you kiped, Steiny."

So I placed the five packs of baseball cards on the crate card table. They fingered the packs like jewelers. "Hey," I said, "it's like the Artful Dodger down here, like in *Oliver Twist* when they go through the stolen stuff."

Rafi winced. "You read that?"

"No. A little. We had a test, remember? But I skipped tons." They winced at me as if I stank. "I know it sounds like boring school stuff, but it's a totally subversive story about pickpockets in London." The word *pickpockets* seemed to spark mild interest, so I continued. "It was written by the same author-guy that wrote *A Christmas Carol*, which had this great scene about thieves in London meeting in a dark cave or something and trading what they steal."

"You can be our librarian," chortled Richard, and Mike asked me to sit down: "Shut up and sit down," he said.

I'd always wondered what guys like this talked about when they were alone. I sat on a crate and listened while they played poker for cigarettes, but no one spoke for maybe ten minutes. Finally Dirk told me, "You should have kiped some comics."

"Maybe next time," I said. "Oh man, it was great. Mike created a diversion by pushing this kid, and I kiped these packs and snuck out."

"You should've kiped something we could sell," sneered Rafi. So Mike reached into his black-leather jacket and laid a shiny golden watch onto the crate. "Twenty bucks," Rafi said with approval.

"Sweet," said Richard.

"For sure," I said. "So what do you guys do down here?" It was a dumb question since I could see what they were doing, but I was sick of the silence.

"We read books," Richard snorted.

"Well it's cool," I said. They turned back to their card game. "This is ultra-ironic," I said, "all this talk about libraries, and we're *under* the damn library now!"

Rafi blew smoke in my face.

"I mean this is really subversive, doing all these things you can't do in school, like smoking and playing cards—right here *underneath* the damn school!"

Marcus glared at me. "You know, we know you think you're really smart with your big words and all, but we all know that *subversive* means *underground*, so shove it."

"I don't think I'm smart! I hate school. I totally hate algebra and the fascist way they teach history, and the gym teachers are ultra-fascist. English is alright I guess, when you get into Huck Finn and all his wild antics... and that Dickens stuff about thieves is sort of cool." They had all turned away, having clearly decided I didn't exist.

So I sat there in silence. But after fifteen minutes in which the only conversation was a few words about what they would steal next, and Rafi saying, "The new Captain Crunch commercial stinks," I nodded at Mike, who snapped his head towards the exit, and slunk off towards the light.

"Your brother wants to see you," my mom said that night. My heart leapt. Ever since my big bro had moved out of our bedroom and into the backyard playroom in tenth grade, the only times I would see him were the occasional family meal and when his TV was broken. And now that he was going away to college, the times would be fewer still.

"Like them?" he smiled. I was staring at his new wire frames.

"Yeah! Definitely. Now all the people I like best wear glasses. Morty, Susie, and you. You look like John Boy Walton."

"That's strange," he said, "since *you're* the writer in the family. C'mere." He reached for a stack of papers he had pulled from his closet while packing. "It's my copy of the mag you and Morty did in sixth grade. *Damn*, it's funny! Autograph it for me?"

It was the most sentimental I'd seen him in all my thirteen years, but you only leave for college once. "Sure!" I said. "Hey, speaking of stories, I've been up to some interesting stuff lately." I told him about the rooftop mountaineering, and the accidental rescue of Mrs. Rosen's cat, and the salt all over Susie's dad's eggs, and the Dime Store heist.

He looked at me with an expression that, I knew from long experience, meant amused disapproval. "Isn't that sort of a waste of time?"

Waste of time? *Waste of time*! Wasn't this the guy whose footsteps I'd followed up onto those dangerous rooftops? Weren't those *his* pranks I had pulled off with perfect fidelity, costing me Susie's approval and my self-respect? Did I even *know* this guy, this long, lean impersonator of my once-cool big brother? Who *was* this guy?

"Got a surprise," this guy said.

"Yeah?" I said coldly. "What?" He flipped the tickets down on the desk. Monterey Jazz Fest, for me and him—a three-day stop on his way up to Berkeley. "Hm, that's alright," I said, not knowing anything about jazz except that my big brother liked it, and that it was jazz sax that wafted from his backyard room when his twelfth-grade friends stayed past midnight playing poker and darts. "*Yeah*," I said. "That's alright." Three-hundred miles up the coast in his convertible two-seater, then two days in San Francisco. "*Very* alright." Damn it, I was giving in easy. *Waste of time*, he had said. *Waste of time*. I fought to stay cool. Five days together, just me and my bro, cruising in the sunshine, blasting the radio, shooting the breeze—*who knew what?* "*Yeah*," I said, "that's alright, bro—*very* alright. *All right! All … riiight!*"

Cousin Sammy

"The very word is an inkblot test. So tell me, Dan: What do *you* think of when you hear the word *Jew*?"

"I think, eighty bucks an hour for free association? Uh oh! There's the look! James' patented, 'Cut out the bullshit and look into my all-knowing eyes' look! *And* the raised eyebrow! Man, I'm getting the works today!"

James measured out just enough grin to acknowledge my perception of myself as a copywriting funnyman, but not enough to let me think I'd deterred him.

"The word, Dan?"

"Say the word, and you'll be free!"

"The Beatles," James sighed. "Now say it out loud."

"I'm a Jew and I'm proud!"

"Good, that's an answer. But tell me, Dan: *Do* you say it out loud? At a crowded restaurant, for instance?"

I shook my head *no*. "I lower my voice."

James nodded as he always did when I made an admission: a gold star on my path to self-knowledge. "Tell me some of the things that make you proud to be a Jew."

"I don't know. Einstein. Groucho. And of course my main man, Sandy Koufax—possibly the greatest pitcher in baseball history. Did you know he wouldn't pitch in the World Series on Yom Kippur?"

"I didn't. That's interesting. Now I want you to dig deeper."

"He said like Charlton Heston as Moses."

"Touché, I'm a Gentile. Now dig deeper, Dan."

"*He said like Darth Vader.*" The clock's ticking hand stuck in anticipation of my response. "Shame," I said. "And betrayal. Man, that light's surrounding your head like an aura."

"We were talking about you, Dan. And Jewishness, and Jews, and why you didn't play football in high school."

"Man, it feels like a confessional in here! You really should be back in the priesthood, James. Here I sit, dizzy and high on a Yom Kippur fast, and I can hear church bells ringing in my ears!"

"I prefer the eye contact in this kind of confessional."

"Well, you're not gonna get it from me, 'cause if you're gonna stare at me with those All-Seeing Eyes, I'm gonna do my client-on-the-couch thing and stare at the ceiling. Did you know you've got eyes like my daughter's? Six years old, and I couldn't fool her for a second. Man, she's a trip. Every word out of her mouth is *Jew this* and *Jew that*. Last Chanukah, it wasn't enough that I got a menorah and presents for the first time ever—she's all, 'Dad, let's make latkes! Dad, let's play dreidel!' And at school, every other kid makes twinkly stars—but with her, it's always the Star Of David! And I mean, *everywhere*. On her art, on her notebook, on the sidewalk in front of our house. And her mom's Episcopalian!"

"Football, Dan?"

"*He sighed like Job.*" My head was floating like a football hanging high against a blue sky. "Why I didn't play football in high school, you mean? Because Sammy Jewboy Dershowitz was my cousin. Listening?"

"It's what I do best."

Which was true. It was how he got me talking so much. Ever since I was a kid, I've seen silence as a vacuum to be filled, like the silence at our dinner table. If I could just make my parents laugh, I felt secure— for the moment, at least.

"I was fourteen years old, a year past the age when a religious Jewish boy *becomes a man*, as they say. Although, for the kids on my block, who were all Jewish-lite, *becoming a man* meant cramming a few Hebrew phrases into your head for a few months, and having a bash at The Sportsman's Lodge. And even *that* was beyond my family's Jewishness, which basically amounted to bagels and lox on Sundays. The neighborhood I grew up in was an assimilating Jewish neighborhood of L.A. a couple miles south of the Borscht Belt on Fairfax, which was Old Country all the way. Smelly delis, Hasidim in black coats and fur hats, wrinkled old people with funny accents.

"The kids I grew up with were plain old bike-riding, sports-playing

American boys, and some were pretty good athletes, too. I was a decent jock, too—*just* decent, unfortunately, because being good in sports was what I wanted most. My whole identity was tied up in sports. And it sure would have helped me through high school. Too many zits, and way too little confidence for girls. *Dun esk*, as my grandpa would say. Unfortunately, I couldn't play the guitar worth beans either. That was Harry Kahn's way out of Nerdville. All those years growing up, while me and the other guys on the block were playing baseball and football and rooftop ditch, Harry was woodshedding in his room, learning guitar. And when he finally came out for high school, *he* was the cool one, not us. And man, that little country boy could play!

"My folks got divorced a few months after my 13th birthday. As if that wasn't awesome enough, my mom and my brother and I had to move down to Long Beach." A girl out on the street was biking into the wind, her legs pumping like pistons. *"Gevalt.* You know, you must be a brilliant headshrinker, James, 'cause I grew up hating Yiddish. Though, not when my grandparents spoke it. But they were from Russia, what was Mom's excuse? I cringed when she spoke it. And my dad cringed, too. Once, at the park, she was taking his picture, with some people nearby. She made some little remark about his big *schnozz*—an affectionate comment—and he lights into her all the way home. 'You sound like a Jew from the ghetto!' and all. And he *had* a big schnozz. So what.

"What a year eighth grade was. I was the new kid in town, literally, and everyone in school knew each other already. Way too brutal for words. I sat in back, ate in the shadows, and dragged my sad ass home to listen to rock in my room. Finally, the last month of school, I made a couple of friends through after-school football. One of them was this jock, Brad Saunders, who lived on my block. A big, tough blond kid, and a monster at football. His dad was a frustrated ex-jock who pushed Brad like a mule. He called Brad *Butkus* for the old linebacker, but we'd call him *Butt Kiss* and pucker our lips. And he'd just smile, though he could kick your ass one-handed if he wanted to. Very cool guy.

110

"So we were all gonna try out for the football team in the fall. Brad was a cinch, but he wanted us all to make the team, so he decided we'd practice all summer. And that's what we did. In the streets, in the park, on the beach ... and that led to other fun stuff. Riding bikes, hanging out. I wasn't *A-list*, but at least I was in. They even took me to Melanie Baker's swim party. And what's this got to do with my cousin Sammy?

"Growing up in the old neighborhood, my cousin Sammy—*Little Sammy Dershowitz*, the big kids on the block always called him—was *the* neighborhood nerd, worse by far than Harry Kahn. Sammy's family were Orthodox Jews, but they might as well have all been from Mars. True, most of us were Jews in that 'hood, but everyone else was a Hebrew Anglo Saxon Protestant, you know? And that Sammy was something. His skin was so pale from staying indoors all the time, studying, you could see the blue of the veins in his arms. I'd call him *Roquefort*, and he'd stick out his tongue and say, 'Wow, a French word from the boy who flunked Spanish.' And he always had that damned yarmulke on. I mean, why not just wear a sign that said, *Jew*? Sammy was my Aunt Esther's kid, my mom's big sister. Mom always made me go over to Sammy's house, 'cause she had this brilliant idea that we should be friends. It was worse than that, they actually thought we *were* friends. Mom was always saying, 'But you like your cousin Sammy.' And I'd say, 'You're trippin', Mom!' Which, Mom *being* Mom, it took two hours to convince her I didn't know what a *trip* was, and I wasn't on drugs. So off I'd go to Sammy's house.

"It was like another world over there. It was always dark, 'cause they always kept the curtains closed. Sammy's father had lost most of his family in the Holocaust, but his mother, Sammy's grandma, survived, because a Hungarian farmer hid her in his barn. But she hated open windows, so the curtains were always closed. And there was serious, dark wooden furniture everywhere, and thick carpets and thick air. Even the smells from the kitchen were thick, like Aunt Esther's brisket of beef and sweet cabbage. They had this beautiful mahogany cabinet with all their Sabbath stuff in it, blue and white china and silver goblets, and a silver pitcher engraved with Hebrew letters.

"Sammy's mom was compulsive about cleaning. You couldn't even tell kids lived there. I'd go over and have nothing to do, and I'd sit on the sofa while Sammy's little sister, Sara, played violin. That Sara was something, a true prodigy. I'd stare with my mouth wide open while she riffed on Tchaikovsky, and she'd catch me gawking and give me this superior little smirk, like, '*I'm* musical, and *you're not.*' Well, maybe I provoked her a little. Like, 'Hey, Cousin Sara, play "Purple Haze"!' Yeah, I provoked her. Anyway, I'd just sit there, bored out of my skull, flipping through my baseball cards and waiting for a chance to go home. Of course, Sammy didn't *have* any cards—though, yeah, once in a while he did show a little interest in mine, looking over my shoulder as if I was handling a rare jewel—which was totally annoying, since he didn't know a home run from a french fry. He'd make some inane remark about how nice the teams' uniforms were, or whether the photograph was 'well composed,' and then his dad would walk by and ask if I'd been studying Hebrew, which was totally absurd and gratuitous, because he knew we weren't religious—which he never failed to remind my dad, before the divorce, when he saw him washing the car on the Sabbath. But he'd ask every time, and every time he'd give me this patronizing smile when I'd say no. Finally, I'd get so bored sitting there that I'd start playing with Sammy. And the funny thing was, he played just like a regular kid! That blew me away. We'd run around playing war, and I'd corner him and move in for the kill—and his dad would say it reminded him of the Battle of Jericho! The man always brought it back to religion. And he was a big-time physicist, even.

"Which brings us back to my fourteenth summer, after eighth grade. Everyone in my new neighborhood was a WASP, and I mean a *WASP*-WASP, not the Jewish WASPs like where I grew up. Aunt Esther would come by to visit her little sister, my mom, every weekend. Mom was having a hard time with the move, and the divorce, and me and my little brother acting out. Aunt Esther would bring a load of food, like her brisket of beef and sweet cabbage, and a box of homemade sugar cookies. And of course she'd bring Sammy, 'cause she and Mom were under the insane delusion that he and I were friends.

"So this one day, about a week before high school was gonna start, we were out in the street playing football: Brad Saunders, and this huge mouth-breather Mark Patterson, and a few other guys who were gonna try out for the team. I was keeping my mouth shut, like always, when Aunt Esther pulled up in her dorky little Plymouth. Then Mom got the brilliant idea of sending Sammy out to play with us. As if we were still ten. As if it didn't matter who saw him. And Sammy didn't like it any better than me. He walked out toward us with his head turned sideways, like he wanted his body to go on and leave his head behind. His legs were so loose, he looked like a mime walking into the wind. And of course, he was wearing his Coke-bottle glasses and yarmulke, and his supercilious grin, maybe slackened a bit when he saw the tough guys I was hanging with. When he finally got out there, he looked at me, lost, and I looked at the ground and mumbled something about his being *Sam*—not *Sammy*, and not 'my *Cousin* Sammy.' So Mark Patterson narrows his eyes, which are just slits in his big beefy face to begin with, and says to Sammy, 'Hey, what's with the beanie?' like it's some great joke. And Sammy just says, 'It's a yarmulke.' Just opens his mouth, and says it! Like that! Like it's the most natural thing in the world! Like, 'Hello, I've got herpes. How about you?'

"So we choose up sides, and Sammy's on my team. What a joke. He goes out for a pass, with his arms and legs flying all around, and stands there like a goof waiting for the ball—which, of course, bounces right off his chest! And I'm dying of shame. Then Brad rifles it in there again, and the ball hits Sammy in the gut and knocks the wind out of him. He doubles over sucking air, and the guys are in stitches—and I'm laughing, too. Which Sammy sees. A little later, my team has the ball, and I drop a pass. Now it's Sammy's turn. 'Nice play!' he yells at me. 'Klutz!' I mean, it's bad enough he rubs it in—but he also has to do it in Yiddish! So the rest of the game, Mark Patterson keeps calling me 'klutz' every time I blow a play.

"So the team with me and Sammy gets creamed. Then Brad decides we have to mix things up to make things fair, and he makes Sammy switch sides with a guy who can play. Now I'm up against Sammy. I go out for a pass, and Sammy's backpedaling like a stork on speed. And he's guarding me close, really sticking to me—as if he gives a damn about football. Brad throws me a pass, and Sammy gets lucky and bats it away. Then he does this goofy little stork dance, smirking at me the way he would when I'd say something dumb about physics.

"So I go out again. Sammy comes running up to guard me, and his yarmulke falls off—and he actually stops to pick it up! You'd have thought he'd dropped the Hope Diamond. Brad zips the ball to me, and I catch it and run for a touchdown. And Sammy's teammates are pissed. Brad slaps me five and says, 'We should give the game ball to the Jewboy!' It didn't sound that bad when he said it—except, there was this gleam in his eye. But I just lowered my eyes and said, yeah.

"Now they have the ball, and I'm guarding Sammy. They have to get to the next lamppost for a first down, and I'm giving him room, because if by some miracle he catches the ball, I can run up and stop him before he gets to the lamppost. Sammy goes out and turns around, and by some miracle, he does catch the ball. So I come barreling in as he turns to run. I'm supposed to just touch him, that's why it's called *touch*. But I don't. I charge in at full speed, and bury my shoulder right in his chest. His head snaps back and his glasses go flying, and you can hear the bones break when his arm hits the street.

"I'd never heard howling like that in my life. His mom comes tearing out of the house wailing like a banshee. I'm waiting to see if she's gonna scream at me, but she tears past me like I don't even exist. But my mom's looking at me from the shadows of the porch, sagging like a doll deflating. 'Cause she knows. She *knows*. And that's the end of my football career. She took me to the hospital to see Sammy that night. He was knocked out on drugs, and his dad told my mom that his arm was broken in two places—and they weren't guaranteeing it'd be good as new."

"Take a deep breath, Dan."

"And do you know what I was doing, while my cousin Sammy was lying on the ground there, howling? I was standing over him yelling, 'Learn how to take a fall, man! Learn to take a fall!'"

James hushed me. "Take a breath, Dan. And another."

I looked up at him through blurry eyes.

"You've been holding that in for a very long time."

The light through the window was intensely white, like some filmmaker's vision of the waiting room between life and death. My head rose up like a floating Chagall fiddler. "Do you know much about Yom Kippur, James? It's about atonement in a major way. To do it really right, you're supposed to go to everyone you've wronged in the past year and tell them you're sorry."

He nodded. "Are you planning to atone?"

I stared at the wall, seeing nothing.

"Where is Sammy now?"

"Here in town, living with his parents in the house he grew up in. With his Orthodox wife, Chava, and their kids: Abe and Solly."

James returned my small grin. "When's the last time you saw your cousin?"

"In the hospital that day. My mom wanted me to be sure I saw him like that."

"I'm sorry, Dan. Our time is up."

I lingered at the doorway, but James eased me out with a definitive touch on the elbow. The waiting room like a church, harboring aching people hoping to be healed. I walked downstairs on shaky legs. The mahogany banister was reassuring, like the solemn wooden furniture in Sammy's house. I opened the door to the white autumn light. Hot dog wrappers swirled at my feet. My stomach growled, and I liked the pain. Jesus was a Jew. Press a thorny crown upon my head.

I slid behind the wheel. My six-year-old angel wanted to fast for Yom Kippur. She'd begged for permission. I told her, kids are exempted from fasting. The next day, she told her mother she was exempted from homework. But at dinnertime, she realized she didn't need our permission. She just crossed her arms and refused to eat. "Please, honey," I begged her. "Just one bite." Finally she agreed to a single mouthful of each thing on her plate.

The car drove me along. How many roads must a man walk down? Dylan was a Jew—*ex*-Jew, that is. Would it have hurt if he'd just stayed a Jew? That mocking smile of Sammy's dad. Why couldn't he let me be a regular, red-blooded American boy? But no. That contemptuous smile when I'd show my ignorance of the *Torah*—like Sara's mocking smile when I'd stare as she played violin like a goddess. Couldn't she have cut me some slack? Why was it up to me to be the strong one, when she was the one who had music, and a strong, loving family behind those drawn curtains?

The car turned onto the familiar street. If I'm not for myself, who will be? But if I'm only for myself, what am I? Twenty years I'd spent adding plates to my armor: college degree, nice wife, great daughter, good job—but I would walk naked into Sammy's house.

Woodsmen

"It was *your* idea to go camping," snapped the dad on a winding back road in search of the campground. He wiped perspiration from heat and embarrassment, braced for the retort.

"*No* it wasn't." The boy's sour glare darted the man's chest.

The dad smiled grimly with comprehension that consoled little for his foolish reliance on a sketchy downloaded road map. "Your mother said you wanted to go camping."

"She was wrong," son declared as if flicking a gnat.

Years before, with a plastic bat fresh from Toys R Us, the boy had swatted ball after ball while his dad "attaboy!'d" at the machine-like consistency of his son. Fifteen now, he still murdered the fat ones. The boy set his chin on a grasshopper knee, gazed at the sunlight that strobed through the redwoods.

"*No* she wasn't *wrong*," the dad brayed. "I said, 'What's Danny into these days?', and she said, 'Camping. The boy loves the outdoors.' So we're camping."

The boy chortled as they rounded another shady bend. "We are?"

"*Yes*," the dad crowed. "There's the sign, behind that huge redwood. Nice job they did of hiding it, no?" He looked at the boy. "Congratulations, Danny, you've perfected your smirk."

"It's *Daniel* now. No one calls me *Danny*."

"*Daniel*," said the father, wincing as if tasting dust in his mouth. "These trees are hundreds of years old ... Daniel. Some are over a thousand, maybe."

Beneath the tires, gravel crunched and twigs snapped. On each side giant redwoods peered down at a father and son going thankfully silent. The dad slowed the car to take in the scene, squinted up in wonder at the trees. "Coast redwoods: *sequoia sempervirens*."

"Latin. Wow."

"Yeah, Latin. Wow. I sure wowed 'em at the bowling alley with my Latin! *Gutter ballus*! Hey, remember batting practice with Hal and

Big Mo? You'd chase balls for hours, then we'd let you hit? Danny? Man, take that damn thing out of your ear!"

"It's an *ear*bud for my *i*Pod, and I'm not ignoring you because of an *i*Pod." The boy glared a bull's-eye at a freckle beneath eyes as intense and demanding as they always had been, but thrillingly vulnerable now, too.

The dad's beset gaze appealed to the treetops for support. "What a spot this is. I reserved it five months ago, and I'm glad I did. Planning ahead, that's the key, Danny Boy."

"That's you, Keith Man."

"*Keith*, Danny?"

"*Danny*," the boy's murmur falling just below the dad's sonar. The dad crunched to a stop at the campsite against a roughhewn timber, cut the engine, clamped the wheel, gritted his teeth and stared at the dash. "Look, Danny—*Daniel*—you're not calling—this guy your mom married—"

"Tom?"

"Yeah. You're not calling him—"

Daniel stretched a flat smile and glanced at his father. When had harsh white crept into his beard? When had his eyes darkened? When had the man shrunk? With a smile implying some secret and superior knowledge, the boy slipped the earbud into the ear that was away from his dad and dialed up the volume, then stepped out into the simmering heat. He measured nearly six-feet-tall when giraffing his neck against the door jamb at his mom's house, and like a sapling he full-faced the sky, closing his eyes to allow the sun's warmth to saturate his face and radiate out to his ears and down his neck, his smile blossoming in the light. The dad approached from the rear to ask for help unloading the truck, but the boy, unaware, pressed his palms together and shot long arms upward, then separated them in controlled slow motion like clock-hands sweeping in opposite directions. The O formed by his father's mouth uttered no reproach, and the man watched in wonder as his son communed with the woods via yoga forms that reached for the sky, waved the clouds, drew wood-sprites from hiding in the tall ferns of a nearby grove and in the high branches of the redwoods themselves. Then the boy, still a novice, crooked a leg to nearly horizontal as his twenty-one-year-old stepbrother had taught him, lost his balance and staggered.

"I don't think I could do that," the dad chuckled. "Not the falling," he hastened to add, "the other."

The boy grimaced at the reference to the stumble, and his dad resumed unloading alone. The man spread the new tent flat on the ground and tossed stakes to the corners. The boy ambled up. "Good spot," said the dad as if allowing his son to listen in on adult conversation. "Nice flat ground, pretty smooth, and a view of the fire ring in case we get bored."

"Sure," the boy mumbled. "Whatevs."

Encouraged by his son's approval, the father turned to him. "It takes four hands to build this thing, D. Good thing you're such a tall son of a gun, you can hold up the center while I bend the poles. How'd you get so tall anyway?" The dad reached for his son's cheek to pinch, but the boy jerked away and twisted a smirk of pained discomfiture and aversion, exactly as his father had feared. The boy grew conscious of the picture-postcard families and happy late-teen couples in nearby campsites and avoided looking at them lest they notice him: there ... in his skin ... on the earth ... with his dad.

The combined weight of the boy's silence, the sky, and the redwoods overwhelmed the father, who directed his son with commando-like gestures as if speech might be fatal. They inserted thin fiberglass poles into tent sleeves and crossed the first two in the center. Then the son, at his father's terse command, held the poles in place like a gangly Atlas as his dad forced the last two poles into their sleeves. They raised the tent and it held its form well, and the man, ceremoniously pounding the last stake into place, congratulated himself on having rehearsed the procedure at home. "Nice job, Dano. Care to go for a hike?"

The boy thought it over. "I just want to chill a while. Soak up the—you know—"

"Atmosphere?" suggested the dad with a pointed grin. "How's English class coming, anyway?"

The boy jerked his head away in annoyance and swung a camp chair into the shade at the edge of the campground. He angled the chair away from the tent and his father, inserted his earbuds and dialed his iPod. The dad looked around as if seeking a witness to his son's disrespect, but the other campers were encased in private bubbles of gladness that seemed as remote as if glimpsed through the wrong end of a telescope. The dad grabbed the other camp chair, set it a few feet from his son's—his ex-wife had advised him that giving the boy space was crucial—and patted the brand new volume of nature poetry he had purchased just for the occasion.

One hour later he turned and declared: "This poetry stuff's great, Danny."

The boy ignored the hint, so the dad pulled his chair closer and tapped his son's arm. The boy pulled out an earbud and directed his gaze along a tangent that grazed his dad's face.

"This Wordsworth guy, Danny, listen: *There was a time when meadow, grove and stream* ... dot dot dot ... *the glory and the freshness of a dream*! I *love* that line! It's like that out here now, isn't it Danny? So fresh and clean? It's nothing like this in the city, is it?"

The boy smiled sourly, as if caught unprepared by a pop quiz.

"Danny, do you even study in school?"

Daniel's face twisted with pain. The dad chastised himself. "I mean," he softened, "poetry is great, son. You really should give it a chance, you know?"

The boy sat as impassively as he had years before when his cloud was set to burst. The dad remembered the sign, popped open a beer and jammed his head down into his shoulders, upset with himself and dismayed by his seed.

They sat silent for hours: iPod and texting on the right, restless reading and journaling on the left, the dad's journal entries staccato bursts following glances at his silent son. The dusk fell cool and sweet, and mosquitos lighted, and the dad swiftly produced a can of mosquito spray from an overstuffed box of camping supplies he had purchased that week. He sprayed his wrists and rubbed them together, then reached a damp wrist towards his son's neck and pressed it against skin as honeyed in hue as pastry crust and sweet smelling from the sun's warmth and a glaze of dried sweat. The son jumped at his father's cold touch on his skin, looked testily at him, and was stunned by the swirl of emotions he found in the man's face—pain among them.

"Sorry, Dad, but you startled me. Thanks, though. You know, Tom said that stuff has DEET in it, it's not good for you. It's like—"

"*Who* is *Tom*?"

The man who's been raising me, the son told himself, pronouncing the syllables in his head as distinctly as a courtroom indictment. "Well," he offered, "this stuff's a lot better than nothing, for sure." He shook the can and looked up at his dad with an effort to reconstitute the trusting gaze of childhood. "How do you—"

But the father mistrusted the malformed gaze. "Like this," he said warily, rubbing his wrists together and applying the spray to forehead, cheeks and neck. "Watch your eyes and nose or you'll mess yourself up."

The son complied, then watched his father for further instructions.

"Hey, let's build that fire now, sport. Why don't you go gather some twigs for... " He gazed into the redwoods with pioneer eyes and at last located the elusive word. "Kindling." The son discerned that his dad had finished issuing instructions, and tromped over to the fringe of the wood to pick up handfuls of small branches and twigs free of moss, as his stepdad had taught him. His father built a criss-crossed structure of fire logs and gestured vaguely at its base. The boy squatted and poked twigs through the openings, taking care to allow room for ventilation. A teenaged girl the next campground over set interested eyes on the boy. The man proudly followed the girl's gaze to his son.

"Want to light it?" the dad asked, nodding at the impressive structure.

The son shrugged ambivalently, noted the disappointment in his father's eyes, then reached compliantly for the proffered lighter. Beneath his father's gaze he knelt and probed the structure's orifices with the lighter until orange flames rendered a castle on fire.

"It reminds me of that jack-o-lantern we carved last—" The dad choked off the sentence: It was his fourteen-year-old stepson with whom he had carved.

The boy whirled like a scratched feral cat, and perceived a blurred impression of the glowing smile of the girl at the next campsite. He set eyes rich with teen code upon her, and she smiled back.

"Danny?" The man looked up from his haunches at the profile of his son's jaw and cheekbones: they were hardening fast, though not yet a man's. "Let's eat." He approached his son, but his son couldn't hear; so he tapped him on the shoulder, and the boy jerked away. The dad pantomimed "take out the earbuds," and when the boy did so, the man added, "I've got your favorite eats," in the coaxing "Come up out of the basement" tone that had worked years before. "Foot-longs."

The boy snapped his gaze at him. "Man, I told you I don't eat flesh!"

The unexpected intensity of the reply knocked the dad's head back and upset his balance. He stumbled backward and tripped on a fire-log and fell down backwards into the fire-ring, collapsing the wood and sending showers of sparks sizzling upwards. He rolled out of the pit howling and ground his back into the dirt to stifle the embers nipping his back. When he finally stopped wriggling, the boy stood over him and reached down his hand to help his dad up; but the man ignored this and panted, from flat on his back: "Stop, drop, and roll, Danny. Remember that if you're ever on fire. You've got to deny oxygen to the fire."

Looking down at his father, an overturned turtle dispensing advice, the boy fought the impulse to laugh; but he did not fight it hard, and quickly succumbed to a giggle that grew into full-throated laughter that rang orange and black like sparks in the night. The night had changed from purple to coal-black, and the boy's laughter transformed into whimpered convulsions of sorrow, elation, freedom, and fear. He turned his gaze to the girl in the next campsite. Her face had darkened in dismay at the father-son discord, and she sat down in a camp chair next to her parents with her back to the boy.

The father set to rebuilding the fire, but the logs were hot and hard to manipulate, and a poor blaze resulted. He rounded his back and bent over the fire and munched defiantly on a foot-long hot dog; then a second, while his son chomped sullenly on a bun stuffed with onions and relish. The night sky deepened, the soft chatter and melancholy guitar chords at nearby campsites diminished along with the campfires, the stars shone cold and silver.

The boy raised his eyes to the multitude of stars, drew cold air and shuddered. His father had disappeared within the embers. The boy felt an impulse to turn to his father. He fought it, faltered, and turned to the man.

"Dad—" the boy started, but the dad's cell phone's ringtone indicated his second wife, and he did not hear.

"Not interrupting a thing, best moment of the day," he said loud and clear, and heedless of his son—who, hearing this, dialed his iPod to shut out the world and seal in Wordsworth's ode to the glory of nature, the freshness of dreams, and thoughts that do often lie too deep for tears.

Night Bloomer

The moon spotlighted Cole and Nick at the edge of the campground with their backs to the fire. Their chortling prompted Cole's dad to creep towards them, but a crunching twig alerted Cole, who jerked his fist down to the side of his leg.

"Whatchya got there, ace?"

"*Vice principal*," drawled Cole, and Nick snickered.

"Nick," said Mr. Crosby, "why don't you go toast marshmallows with Cole's mom."

Cole said: "Harsh, Dad! Isn't *toasting marshmallows* some old-school putdown?"

Mr. Crosby's dark look made Nick choke back his laugh. "Sounds good, Mr. C. For some reason I'm starving."

"For some reason."

Mr. Crosby stared after as Nick walked away, and turned back just as Cole was reaching his arm back to hurl something into the trees. He grabbed Cole's wrist before he could.

"You're hurting me."

"Bull."

Cole comically whined, "My pitching career!"

Mr. Crosby winced: Cole had quit the team a year before. "What's in your hand?"

Cole jerked his arm, his dad clasped his wrist tighter.

"Cole."

"Dad."

"What's in your hand?"

"In my hand, in my head! In my backpack and drawers!"

Cole's wrist had thickened as a tree's trunk thickens. He'd have been a great pitcher.

Mr. Crosby stared down. "I love you," he said. A plain declaration, still holding the wrist.

"You're a fascist," said Cole, but his seething words broke up even as he released them.

Cole's pulse tattooed the skin of his father's palm, while his gaze, fierce and frightened, explored his dad's eyes.

His dad's hand unfurled like a night-blooming flower.

A Man Forbid

"Sleep shall neither night nor day
Hang upon his penthouse lid.
He shall live a man forbid."
~ Weird Sister, *Macbeth*

Soil rich black and moist yearned like woman awaiting the seed. The sleeper's lips trembled as the dreamer beheld a single seedling emerging from the soil, teardrop leaves of luminous green arching out from its crotch, the soil black and moist as the gigantic wedges of cake in the magazine ads his mother would paste to the fridge like a dream of home life. In these ads the cake was dark and moist and layered with buttercream, and the edge of the fork sliced into the cake the way the dreaming man's hoe had cut into the rain-sodden soil of the vegetable garden an hour before. The dreamer's mother had made these cakes as a Sunday treat when the dreamer was small and there were still four at home, and he'd gorged on them 'til his stomach ached. Then, in the hot nasty summer when he was fourteen and there were just the two of them left, she made them all week, and he shunned them to shun her, and he counted out loud each bite that she took, and when he did that she would lower her head to eat in a shamed, petulant way, chewing like a cow masticating; then, when she'd finish, he'd skateboard around the corner and take one toke on a joint and one pull on a beer for each of her bites. In the dream she wore the orange-and-yellow flowery thing she called a "muumuu" because it made her feel as if she were in Hawaii, persisting in doing so despite Iris's snide, "It's a *dress*, Mama," despite her husband calling it a horse blanket, despite him calling it a tent at age twelve to raise Papa's bitter smile. He worked hard every night to copy that smile in the mirror, and when Papa left for good, he perfected it without trying. In the dream his mother was thirty-five or so, yellow-haired, double-chinned, and shapeless in her muumuu, standing on the bare ground of an ill-defined park scooping moist black earth with her dish-red hands, reaching out mounds of earth to him with a smile innocent of the heartaches to come: the smile he

126

remembered from when he was four. "Do you like it, Mackey? Do you like it again?" He moaned, "I like it, Mama," and reached out

but the guard smashed his baton against the heavy metal lock-plate and Mack shot up screaming. Officer Padik was as big as an offensive lineman, with a round face slitted by eyes that gleamed and thin lips that curled with the pleasure of having made Mack scream. Mack sat up at an acute angle to the officer, cradled his face in cracked red hands, blinked tears from his eyes. Angered by the lack of eye contact, the guard strummed his baton across the bars the way Mack at fourteen had clattered the wrought-iron fences in "the nice folks' neighborhood" with his bat, awakening weekend sleepers. One silver-haired man growled "barefoot trash," and Mack slashed his tires and fled into the woods, where his friends raised their beers to anoint "Mack The Knife." "Sleeping in the daytime?" the guard said with mock shock. "How the hell you gonna get ahead in life if you sleep in the daytime?" The guard puffed up with his wit, but Mack remained mute as a pill bug. "Hey, I'm *talk*ing to you!" The officer banged the door, and Mack looked up at him through red eyes sunk deep into sockets as wide and deep as goldfish bowls. The guard probed the prisoner's countenance for dissent, but there had been no dissent since Mack's first night in jail three years before, when the guard had delivered two expert blows to his shins with his baton as he slept, "expert" in that they delivered great pain without any telltale fracturing of bone. "Lemme show you something," said the guard. Mack stepped gingerly to the bars, and the guard thrust a wallet photograph at his face. "She's beautiful. Isn't she?" It was the shiny black extended-cab pickup that the officer had purchased two months before. "That didn't come from sleeping all day." Officer Padik snorted contemptuously and peered down at Mack. "Got a surprise for you, Mack. You're gonna get a new roommate! And you are really gonna like this one, Mack—a new friend to have pillow talk with, a person to tell your secrets to. Hell, Mackey, you are such a good friend."
But the roommate wasn't due for several more days, and the delay

had the effect that Officer Padik intended, for Mack was chronically jumpy from lack of sleep to begin with, and this new anxiety wore his nerves down to wires. In the mess hall, in the library, in the exercise yard, he jerked his head at fellow prisoners in the suspicion that they knew the nature of the new torment that awaited him and were laughing at him. Only in the vegetable garden did he find any peace. There he knelt to the rain-sodden soil and worked it with his trowel, feeling himself the kindly god of the small patch of earth shadowed by his body. He had a mellow gardening friend known as Gen'ul G, an enormous reformed dealer from Hunter's Point who likewise sought solace in the soil. Everything the big man knew about gardening he had learned from Mack, who had learned an enormous amount about the cultivation of veggies, and weed, in his youth in the foothills of the Ozarks. G passed behind Mack with a hoe on his shoulder, and when his enormous shadow covered Mack's little kingdom, Mack sprang up into a knife-fighter's crouch with the trowel as his weapon. Gen'ul G laughed: "Mac The Trowel, what a fool."

Mack lay on his back like a vampire in his coffin, arms folded across his chest, neck stiff as rigor mortis. He failed to fall asleep for two hours, then dreamt that a shadow, black and shapeless as a vampire's cloak, or an oil slick, or a black ectoplasm, or a giant bat ray, or Gen'ul G's shadow, hovered over his head and began to descend as if to smother him. He shot up again, and slept no more that night.

Officer Padik shoved the new roommate into the cell the next morning. He was thin and thirtyish, with sallow, pock-marked cheeks, soft, dewy eyes in black sockets, and hair dyed artificially black. "You guys are gonna get along like peas in a pod," Officer Padik snurfled, "like Anthony and Cleopatra. Just don't turn your backs on each other." He closed the cell gently in a comic burlesque of a kindly father closing his sons' bedroom door for the night, blew a soft kiss through the bars and stepped away—then whirled and crashed his baton against the door. The new guy jumped and shrieked.

Mack judged Anthony to be harmless due to his scrawny build, nervousness that was extreme even for a new guy, and especially his eyes. Mack had known dangerous men on the streets of the Tenderloin and in Golden Gate Park, where he'd made his last camp, and this guy's eyes lacked their menacing glint.

And then the guy started talking in a thin, high voice, treating time as a terrifying void he must cram full of words: "Alright, so, um, like, well—and what are *you* in for? Uh huh, uh huh. Okay, never mind! That was rude of me to ask, just please don't be angry, oh *please*, honey, won't you cut me some slack? I mean, imagine how *I* feel right now. I mean, look: I bet the new meat *always* chatters like this. Oh, they do? Of *course* they do, *sure* they do, all chatter-chat-chat, hey, that's *nor*mal, that's my own personal normally abnormal way anyway, I just roll like that, I chatter like a chipmunk, got to fill my cheeks—" a delicate hand covering a naughty mouth— "okay, let me start over. Okay. I mean, look. My god. Honestly! And what the hell else is there to do in a place like this except talk talk talk? A place like this!" Anthony laughed hysterically. "As if there actually are *places like this*! Well, I suppose we could—I don't know … *de*corate, maybe! I mean, gawd, these white walls are just *gor*geous with those cute cracks in the plaster, and that picture of—ooh, that's sort of like—a stock car, right? Wow, I'm rooming with the Duke Of Hazzard! That's a joke, don't kill me! Omigod, oh god, I am gonna *die* in here!" Anthony snuffled hysterically, gasped for air, then stood up straight and raised his chin in an attitude of perfect dignity. "No, honey, I assure you: you most definitely did NOT get a fruitcake for your cellmate. A cellmate! Omigod, oh my sweet fucking god, I'm a cellmate in a prison, and I am going to die! Thank you, you're sweet. Oh, and you gave me a clean tissue, too! Stop looking at me, I was making a joke!" Snufflling turned to sobbing. "I just wanted to say that you're a fine host, a real country gentleman, and that is no—oh, what's the damn word? Aspersion! That is no aspersion on your country background—my god, I should talk, I'm from Hicksville, Oregon, that's just rednecks with guns. Oh please, god, please, would you please stop looking at me with those cold blue eyes, I don't even know where you're from! And if I did know, I'd love it, I love everyone from wherever they come from, don't you get it, you dope? So where *do* you come from? Oklahoma? No? Texas? No? Thank *gawd* it's not Texas! Arkansas? I knew it! Hey, a president came from there, that's nothing to be ashamed of. Don't look at me like that! You're killing me," between sobs, "I didn't say there's anything wrong with that at all, I said just the opposite in fact, if you'd care to look at the record. Help me, oh god, I'm gonna be sick! I need cigarettes! Thank you ... you're a true gentleman." A furtive hush: "Hey. Do you know how to get some coke in this place? Crack, maybe? What's that shrug mean, no, you can't get it, or no, you don't trust me? Never mind, I agree: we just met; we're not there yet. *Sigh.* You know, I could get those things out on Polk Street with a snap of my fingers ... I'm not bad looking, though this lighting's from hell. I could ... you know ... *do* things ... Christ, would you stop looking at me like that!"

"I'm listening to you."

"Oh yeah?" Anthony peered at Mack through narrowed eyes. "Then listen to this. I may be queer, but nobody—and I mean, *nobody*—fucks with me. The last time a john tried to steal my wallet I stuck him right in the ass with a big fucking pair of kitchen scissors, so—omigod, sit down!" Anthony scuttled backwards and balled himself against the wall on his cot. "Please sit down," he snuffled, "I was kidding, just kidding! God, please get me out of this place!" Anthony closed his eyes and shivered all over, then squeaked up in a constricted little voice that barely made it all the way through his windpipe: "Help me, man. I am gonna get *mur*dered in here!"

Mack knit his brow and pondered the circumstances. "No," he said soberly. "You're not. You got me and G, he's got pull with the brothers, we give 'em extra veg from the garden. It's supposed to go to some restaurant or something, but ... Listen, you'll be cool. You won't even have to—"

"Oh god, I love you! Omigod, think of that—*I* love a cracker! In bed!" Anthony leaned back in alarm. "Omigod, that's a joke! Honey, don't you even know me by now?" Mack sat back down, and Anthony, calming himself with a great effort, subdued his tone. "So what did you object to, anyway: the *cracker*, or the bed? Ah, you smiled! See, I *knew* you could smile. You've just gotta know me, sugar. Every time I open my big pretty mouth it gets me in trouble—oops, I did it again!" he sang as Britney Spears. "Change the subject fast, ladybird!" Anthony straightened his back, crossed slender legs and skinny arms and mimed holding a cigarette like a cocktail party hostess. "Okay, new topic. So tell me, Arky. Do you like marbles?"

"What?"

"Or cheetahs? Or Cheetos? Or—oh, Christ, I don't know, do you like—" Anthony spiraled his fingers as if to pluck conversational fruit from a vine— "antelopes? Or artichokes? Or spring rolls, maybe? There's a Vietnamese place on O'Farrell, and the guy at the counter pretends he's straight, but we all know he's queer as a flamingo taquito. And the spring rolls in there—"

Hours later, Anthony was still talking.

"Jesus," said Mack, "you are one wired dude."

"Hey, I'm a... wired sister!" trilled Anthony.

"Yeah, well, Wired Sister, I need some sleep big time."

Anthony leaned across the space separating the cots. "If I sleep I'll die."

"I'll die if I don't."

In a tremulous hush the new prisoner said, "It's scary in here. Don't you think I could sort of—you know—get under the covers with you, snuggle up a little, like a sleepover thing—"

"*No.*"

With stiff-necked dignity the new guy replied, "Then goodnight, Mister... I didn't catch your last name?"

"Betts. Mack B." Mack initiated a standard firm handshake, warning Anthony with a hard gaze to respond in kind. "Now go to sleep, man."

Anthony lay flat on his back with eyes open. He continued to talk, but reduced the volume of the chatter he directed at the phantoms in the air such that Mack could tune it out like a neighbor's radio.

But Mack couldn't sleep. In the post-midnight stillness his cellmate's incessant murmuring came into sharp focus like conversation on the other side of a thin flophouse wall, and he couldn't tune out the endless stream of words. "Shut up," he barked, but that switched on muffled sobbing, so he grumbled "Forget it" and clamped his eyes shut. He fell asleep hours later, and dreamed that he lay in Golden Gate Park, in the pup-tent-sized hollow beneath a gnarled tree that he and Janine had called home for three months, tearing down camp every morning before the park gardeners showed up, making camp at sundown when the civvies were gone. They had just shot up, and he lay face down on his bedroll, resting his splotched face on the puffed-up sleeve of the jacket he'd scored at Goodwill, as the drug came on. "Hey," Janine said with the feather-soft murmur, ragged at the edge, that signaled her desire and aroused his, and he smiled at her—oh, how she loved how his smile raised the plunging edges of his mustache and made him look boyish. In the dim twilight she looked closer to her actual age, twenty-eight, than the leathery forty she appeared in bright daylight, and her dimpled cuteness and mini-Oreo eyes filled him with wild tenderness. He rolled onto his back and closed his eyes in anticipation of receiving her body—but a sudden premonition of evil opened his eyes to the killer from *Psycho* standing above him with his arm raised high—but it wasn't a knife, but a huge pair of scissors gleaming in the darkness, and it wasn't a movie-killer, but Anthony plunging the scissors down towards his heart.

He rolled over violently before the scissors could land, arousing Anthony from a weak doze. "What's wrong?" Anthony murmured in a concerned parental tone. Mack stared at him in a catatonic daze, and Anthony insinuated himself to a standing position and took a tentative step across the floor like a tightrope walker; when Mack didn't move, he slide-stepped once more and stood next to his cellmate. Mack looked up at Anthony. The harsh white light from the naked bulb in the corridor directly across from the cell illuminated his deep-black death's-head eye sockets. Anthony lowered himself with the caution of a bomb-squad technician and the delicacy of a ballerina and laid a skeletal arm around Mack's shoulders. Mack threw it off in reflexive revulsion.

"I understand," said Anthony, raising his chin with formal dignity. "It'll be alright, baby." He touched a soothing finger to his lips. "If you need me, just say so. I don't ever sleep, really."

So Mack laid back down and tightened his face in a grim mask fit to scare away demons. He sang Johnny Cash and Merle Haggard tunes in his head for an hour and more, then slept, then dreamed. In the dream he was twelve again, asleep before dawn, and the twelve-year-old sleeper was dreaming too, and in this dream within a dream he was walking through the nice folks' neighborhood on the way to the good ball yard with its grass infield, raised pitcher's mound, and fenced outfield, walking in the exact center of the street, inhaling the sweet alyssum that grew along the wrought-iron fences of the nice folks' homes; but he didn't dare turn his face to the blossoms, but looked straight ahead, shielding his eyes from the blinding white light that pervaded the air and burned his lungs. On an impulse he took off running, and kept running until he reached a cool green field that was not the ball field, but was the ball field. His friend John was there, sitting on his bike. Why oh why had he turned against John? Or was it the reverse? And all of a sudden, it no longer mattered—for John, swathed in golden light, smiled at him, and he dared smile back. But in the outer dream, in which he dreamed about a dreamer, his father, in the power-company hard hat he wore during Mackey's twelfth summer, shook him hard by the shoulders. "Get up, candy ass. If I can get myself out of bed at this hour, you sure as hell can too," and the twelve-year-old dreamer looked up at his father with wide-dish eyes and a wide-opened mouth to speak the words he had never dared—

Officer Padik banged the baton on the lock plate and strummed the bars. "Get up, punks!" His smile bloomed when the cellmates raised themselves to a bleary-eyed sit.

In the library was a psychology section comprised of two textbooks, neither of which answered Mack's desperate question: How to resume a truncated dream? A middle-aged long-timer with some nebulous claim of a connection to Stanford—a claim supported by his scholarly appearance: spectral frame, wispy chin, weak blue eyes that beamed through round wire-frames with the implication that the man occupied a private world of knowledge and wisdom to which he'd conduct you, if you were worthy and capable (highly doubtful)—stroked his chin and allowed that, "Yes, certainly, there must be an answer to this fascinating question which has challenged thinkers and seekers throughout the ages. Of course, in ancient Greece, in *The Odyssey*, as you know… " (he chuckled with gentle irony at the notion that Mack would know) "reference is made to the lotus eaters, which is not discordant with historical fact—for there is, indeed, evidence that the ancient Greeks, lofty thinkers and dreamers that they were, used opium, *shhhhh*—" (a finger to the man's thin parched lips stifled a chuckle at the mention of one of the multitude of psychotropic drugs for the possession of which he had been imprisoned) "used opium, aka nepenthe—as in, 'quaff this nepenthe, help me forget my lost Lenore'—'The Raven'—of course!—a drug to induce forgetfulness… nepenthe… and is that not akin to dreaming, i.e., shutting out external stimuli, allowing the subconscious mind to roam freely? Ah! We're getting somewhere! A plausible means to reenter dreams! Perpend: For, as I say, the ancient Greeks utilized various psychotropic drugs as a means of accessing certain portals of the mind, and these *portals*, we may call them, may allow access to various points in the mind, points of consciousness; and studies suggest—*reveal!* that the situs of memory can be geographically mapped in the brain, to the hippocampus—which is *not* a college for hippopotami!" A wild chuckle. "And is a dream, once dreamed, not a memory, too? And so, student, does it not stand to reason that memories themselves can be mapped, accessed, and retrieved from definite sites, that's s-i-t-e-s? Now, if you will permit me a digression. If we consider certain mind-expanding substances as somewhat analgous to training wheels on a bike—*id est*, a training device that can ultimately be dispensed with once the desired skill is attained… if you think, for instance, of a musician—a pianist, say, practicing blindfolded in order to deepen his purely aural awareness of the music... the subtle intonations, reverberations, undertones, harmonics... Grigorian chants come to mind, as do—"

Mack slipped away in disappointment and disgust with Anthony trailing five feet behind: not close enough to invite a beating by other inmates, necessarily, but close enough for Anthony to experience the illusion of safety.

Mack laid himself down, determined to return to the bright-green ball field of his dream and his lost friend John. He lay for hours in the coffined vampire position trying various methods of falling asleep. Singing Merle Haggard to himself couldn't do it. Johnny Cash couldn't do it—and to his horror, he discovered that he couldn't recall the words to "Long Black Veil," though he'd sung himself to sleep with the song hundreds of times. So he tried to visualize the most soothing image he could think of, the bright-green mustard seedlings that were just then emerging in his prison garden plot; but every time he managed to summon a clear image, he was snapped out of his reverie by the terrified mutterings of his cellmate, who lay flat on his back staring at the ceiling as the harsh white light of the corridor filled the deep bowls and crevices of his face. Since Mack couldn't tune out Anthony he tried the opposite and tuned into his rambling the way he had strained as a kid to hear *America's Most Wanted* or *COPS* through the wall of his parents' room after bedtime. That worked for a while, for his mind was drawn away from itself by Anthony's fragmented mumbling about knives in the ass and thieving johns and god! don't! no!—but then he was jolted into full wakefulness by the recollection of his father snapping, "Get to fuckin' sleep in there!", the frequent prelude to the sound of angry rutting. So he counted monster trucks crushing Civics, but the trucks dissolved into switchblade knives that hung in midair dripping blood onto his black garden plot, and then the knives became blood-dripping scissors, and the lack of sleep became the physical pain of the skin of his face flaking like roast pork sliced from the bone.

He shot upright, and realized that he had been dreaming of

himself lying there awake.

Hours later he fell back to sleep and dreamed that he wore a golden crown like the one from his fifth-birthday party, when his dad had passed through the living room snorting, "We all know who's the king around here." But in the dream he was twelve, not five, and he met John again on the grass of the ball field. He hailed "King John!" but John charged off into the woods on his bike, so Mackey took off after him on bare feet that flew over the wet grass, and dove into the woods as if sliding head-first into second base, landing on... the bed of soft leaves that Janine laid down beneath their bedrolls in their little encampment in the park every night. "Safe," said Janine, but there was mockery on her lips and a reproachful hardness in small black eyes, the look of being too long without scag: which was always *his* fault: she could have been a singer, hell, she'd received beer money and twenty bucks cash singing R&B with a band in Stockton last year, and she hadn't even had to put out—and what the hell was she doing with a loser like him! C'mon, Janine, he told her, flopping onto his back and flashing the grin that she couldn't resist. But she threw her chin up and shook her head no! no! no!, the terror of being without the drug arousing hysterical laughter that melted into weeping. C'mon, baby, he said, sitting up and wrapping his arms around her heaving body, softly stroking her musty hair. She calmed down, cocked her head at him in a calculating way and pushed him back by the chest and down onto the bedroll, and climbed up onto him—but her eyes looked off to the kayak-sized hollow a few feet from theirs in which a college dropout from Michigan slept, he'd been camping there for weeks. Mack saw the look and woke up with cold sweats.

He had one tab of acid. It had cost him four bunches of baby carrots, a prized artichoke, five packs of cigarettes and twelve dollars cash, and he'd saved it for a special occasion. The pseudo-Stanford man had spoken of reentering dreams by psychotropic means, and it seemed worth a shot. He swallowed the tab and laid down to wait to come on—but the exhaustion from two-plus sleepless nights overcame him, and he lapsed quickly into sleep. Whether he came on to the drug before he dreamt or no, he was back in the park and Janine was atop him. She held a forty-ounce can of malt liquor over her head, and extended her tongue below the mouth of the can to catch the last precious drops, then threw the can onto a pile of empties. She lowered her mouth to his ear and softly whispered "loser," which filled him with a blend of anger and desire. She lifted herself up laughing hysterically, shuddered violently and threw her head back. She seemed far above him even before her neck began telescoping upward like Alice's after eating the cake, and when her head was near the canopy of the eucalyptus trees, she gazed down with red dragon eyes at the kid from Michigan sleeping nearby. Then she was herself again, sexy and cute, and she rocked her hips upon him, hard. He tried to pull her down to maneuver her into the bedroll, but she thrust a stop-sign hand in his face, then lowered her mouth to his ear and said, in a soft, ragged hush: "He's got scag, man. That stinking slumming rich boy's been holding out on us, and we've fed him for weeks. And you kept him from getting rolled by those punks! You know," she said, modulating down to a soft key, "he's been eyeing me, man—when you're not around. You know, he is kind of cute." She flicked his ear with her tongue, breathed warmth into his ear. "Called you a cracker." What a sweet voice she had! And how sweet she smelled—somehow, although homeless, she somehow managed to smell nice. Then she convulsed from the agony of twenty-one hours without smack, seized the neck of his jacket and lifted his head, shook it up and down in rhythm to words barked through ragged tears: "What do you care, man! You never do nothing for me, nothing! And you say you're a man!" He reached up to grab her but was sluggish from the booze, and she broke away with a fearsome "No!" and rolled off him, turned her back to him and gazed suggestively at the college kid sleeping in the hollow. A black adder within constricted Mack's intestines and squeezed them towards bursting. Mack moaned aloud, rolled his head desperately, set bleary eyes on a gleaming object. His switchblade. She had opened it for him, laid it next to his hand.

And then he remembered.

Fig Tree Gazing

Morton Vickery needed a friend. Not a wifely friend, he had one of those, nor a soft-handed friend for discussing the market, there were columns of those in his accountancy firm. What Morton dreamed of, as he stared in the mirror and pressed palms together to make his pecs quicken like tiny mice scurrying beneath paper skin, was a got-your-back, take-no-prisoners, rough-and-ready, tough-yet-tender, red-blooded, sensitive, manly-man friend—the kind he'd not had in forty-five years of life.

"You need to come to *bed*, Morton."

"I'll come to bed when I'm ready, Mother." The sharpness of his own voice surprised Morton, and surprise turned to shock when he grew fully conscious that it was not his mom but his wife who had just spoken to him in the chilly tone that his mother had utilized to subdue him during his brief rebellious phase at age twelve. Morton directed his gaze beyond the half-closed bathroom door to Millie, who looked spectral in the dim light of the bedroom in her loose-fitting, full-length pioneer nightie with its dull white glow. This time, for once, Morton held her dark gaze, and set his jaw against a small scowl that conveyed menace along with something new: there, glimmering in the depths of his wife's black eyes like a remote star, Morton discerned a pinprick of fear. Millie thrust the point of her chin at her husband and withdrew from his presence like a frightened wraith fast-fleeing a torch. Morton turned a wry smile to the mirror and stroked his smooth chin—and, like an adolescent just beginning to discover himself, admired the clean, sharp line of his jaw. There would be no sex, but that was the norm, and the certainty of the knowledge freed Morton's mind. So when Millie snapped off the bedside lamp and pointedly turned her back to her husband, Morton felt empowered to keep the laptop humming despite his wife's preference for a womb-dark, silent room, and stared into its campfire glow.

Camping, that was it—the way to meet men. Morton ("Mort,"

138

never) had not camped since Boy Scouts, had rarely even hiked; but you never forgot the skills, he decided. Nor, he realized, could you forget the bad parts: the loathing he'd felt for his spindly teen legs exposed by khaki shorts, the shame of padding past neighborhood toughs while wearing those awful green knee stockings, the discomfort and isolation he'd felt mouthing prayers with fading reverence in the fellowship circle, and the ache in his gut when he caught the pastor's reproachful glare.

Even so.

"Camping," he said right out loud, to spite the tension that cut through the darkness. "I'd love to go camping. I'd love to, dammit," uttering the uncharacteristic expletive in an awkward low hush. The only answer was the snap of the bedsheet being pulled tight. "I should ask Hank, Bill's contractor friend." Morton waited for Millie to invite herself along. She remained as silent as stone. "He's a nice guy," said Morton, "an *in*teresting guy," the *in*teresting a coded challenge. "I should call him. I will."

"*Hank*," Mille sneered.

"Right," Morton answered. "I'll call him for sure."

Morton usually went to bed long after Millie. It had been so for years, the gap between their bedtimes ever increasing. Years before, when their matrimonial ship reached the doldrums, he had sounded her by deliberately leaving the bills for late at night, and she had responded with a perfunctory sigh before diving into her mystery novels, celebrating the completion of each chapter with a chocolate from a box she hid from Morton's view on the bottom shelf of her bedstand. Then, in the heady days of the bull market, he'd convinced her that he needed to study the market late at night to get a jump on the next day's trading. She'd agreed to that, too. The payoff had been the Lexus, private schools for their daughter (now at Brown), and their stylish hilltop home with a view of Mount Tam. So much discomfort avoided this way: Was it he? Was it she? Who was to blame for the awkward lovemaking, frustration, confusion?

They'd married in college, in the church they'd grown up in. Each was the first lover of the other, and neither could carry half of the load. Though she had tried once. In a burst of enthusiasm two years into the marriage, she had experimented with new perfumes and hairstyles, and lingerie just as daring, and not a jot more, than would be allowed by the hard, disembodied voices and disapproving gazes of parents and priests. It made no difference, for work and money were all his delight.

Even so the baby had come. He had joked that it had been an immaculate conception, and she had bristled at the sacrilege as well as the breach of their tacit taboo against alluding to the infrequency of their lovemaking. At this point he had taken the lead in addressing their problem—though "problem" was a forbidden word—for he loved the child, and so loved the woman who had brought her forth. With the tentativeness of a bomb squad technician, he'd mumbled something about new positions. She'd gritted her teeth until he was done. Then he discreetly obtained a book about sex—overly clinical, not much fun—and muttered half-hearted incantations to the air about "pelvic muscles" and "Kegel exercises," and she had tearfully thrown the book at the wall and muttered with spite: "You try it, too." After that he'd retreated to his home office, where he studied the market until long after midnight while she prayed that he was not looking at porn. Finally, one soft Sunday afternoon after church, as they sat on a bench on the elevated redwood deck outside their bedroom, they looked as one at a parting of silvery clouds overhead. Contrary to custom they remained on the bench, leaving undisturbed the wedding-cake-white spread on their king-sized bed even though this was the appointed time for conjugal relations. They gazed at the clouds as if of one mind and watched their sex-life drift softly away. Since then he had traded stocks in peace, and she had busied herself with handiwork of all kinds, exchanging with relief the silk pajamas she had purchased at Nordstrom in the flush of new wifehood for the ankle-length nightie she had worn in high school, adorned with puff balls and white like surrender.

"What are you doing in there Morton?" Millie's voice rang with alarm, for the bathroom door was all the way closed.

"You know, Millie, it's a*maz*ing how much you sound like my mother." The excitement of conflict electrified his voice.

"And what were you doing in the bathroom when she said that, Morton?" Her forced laughter rattled like bones.

"Jesus, Millie, why don't you just come in and see?" The blasphemous note sounded strained to Morton himself. He thrust the door open, revealing himself in pajama pants but no top, and he resisted the impulse, ingrained at adolescence, to cover his hairless chest with his arms. She gaped like a teen unexpectedly glimpsing a teacher half naked at a pool, and he focused his gaze on the full lower lip that had driven him wild in church at sixteen, now hanging like fruit to be picked, and picked hard.

"Is that how your new friend talks?" Maternal disapproval did not obliterate a note of intrigue in her voice.

"Maybe." Morton set his jaw and turned again to the mirror, and curled his newly-bought dumbbells with increased vigor.

Millie studied his frame. Thin, yes, but strong enough to make him a serviceable carrier of groceries, backyard gardener, and power-walking companion on the leafy roads that entwined their house. She was grateful that he had never gotten fat, did not smoke or drink, would not likely die early and leave her alone. She was grateful, too, that he gave the church ladies no basis for gossip.

"Why so obsessed with your body all of a sudden?" More bone-rattling laughter. "Trying to look good for your new friend?"

"Yes, Millie. I'm trying to look good for my friend."

Morton camped at first with Bill and Hank, and then with Hank only, returning energized with a wisp of beard and the scent of wood-smoke and pine clinging to his body. The aroma aroused Millie's sense of smell even as it alarmed her like the perfume of an Other Woman. Morton kayaked with Hank on the Russian River, hiked the woods of Sonoma, climbed rocks in the mountains of Santa Cruz. While he was gone, Millie resisted, then yielded to, the gnawing urge to search his computer for porn, and his emails for hints of an affair. In a secret place she could not understand she was mildly disappointed not to find either, though the pictures of Morton with Hank had clutched at her heart with falcon talons. This, then, was Hank: a huskier, heartier version of Morton himself, with sun-burnished skin and gleaming eyes narrowed as if sighting a hawk, and an iron beard that was full but well groomed. In one picture, Hank wound a woodcutter arm around the narrow shoulders of Morton, whose broad smile, unfamiliar to Millie or maybe forgotten, seemed that of a giddy girlfriend.

"Have you seen this movie?" Millie asked with rehearsed nonchalance as her husband dragged his duffle into the house late at night. "*Brokeback Mountain*." She did not look up lest her face signal the ruse.

Morton was clever as an accountant, clever as an investor, and clever now in discerning her motive. "No, Millie, but I'd like to. Two men getting it on in the wild. Sounds awesome."

"I think it's disgusting," she said with fear and conviction, clicking the film off as he passed by.

She sought solace in cleaning. Their home was built of rectilinear hardwood cut into a hillside, and the entire south wall of the living room was a floor-to-ceiling picture-window affording a view of wooded hills and valleys and the peak of Mount Tam, which legend and Millie's own anxious imagination affirmed to be the profile of a flowing-haired lady lying on her back. The view was her glory, and though she had kept the window clean always she now cleaned it daily, stretching, reaching, bending in her cotton sweats, glorying in the litheness of long slender limbs tracing graceful arcs upon the glass. The sunlight glinted diamond-hard off the glass while a red-tailed hawk cruised a valley for prey. An impulse jolted Millie to clean in the nude. She peeled off her clothes and stretched her limbs to the sun and the hawk, but stomach acid rose up and gagged her. She lowered herself onto the clean, thick, white pile carpet and sat there lightheaded and pressed her eyes shut, feeling as if her head would explode. She gathered herself, reviling herself for surrendering to the impulse, but even more for her guilt. So, with the excitement of the virgin bride who twenty years before had lifted the bed-sheet to glimpse her sleeping newlywed husband in the nude, she clutched the luxuriant carpet with her toes.

Millie retreated to the comfort of batches of cookies she baked for her book club, reserving dozens for solitary times when she'd fill her mouth with sweetness and warmth and softness like thighs. She chewed with luxurious thoroughness but denied herself the satisfaction of swallowing, instead disgorging a chunky brown sludge into paper bags she buried in the compost bin. Sometimes she'd give in and swallow a bite and then a whole cookie, and then she'd stick a stiletto finger down her throat to purge herself of vomit and mucus and tears of self-loathing, kneeling at the toilet like a wretched penitent enfolded in self-abasement.

Even though she was thin, even though the house clean, her husband continued adventuring with Hank. In early spring the two rafted for three days, and Morton returned with coppery cheeks and a proud, boyish smile framed by a thin new growth of beard. She had often teased him for his inability to grow a full beard, but lacked the will to do so now as she sat deflated on the couch staring through the TV, her knees hiked to her chin, her stocking feet resting on the chrome-and-steel coffee table, her pioneer PJ's riding up slender, carved calves above white sweat socks. Her nose bunny-quivered at Morton's musky scent, and though she did not look up at him, she sensed him staring down at her. He walked over on hardened legs and squeezed her big toe, chuckling with derision at the sweat socks. Then he took a long steaming shower during which he sang spirited rock songs in a croaking, flat voice that was just as flat but much less subdued than it had been at church before he'd ceased the charade and stopped going. She glided to the door, leaned her back up against it and rubbed up and down it like a cat until the croaking was done, and then she flitted away like a finch.

There was a feral cat that haunted the deck. His coat was smoky grey, his haunches and shoulder muscles rippled when he sauntered along the wooden rail surrounding the deck, and he exuded supreme confidence and superior knowledge in a gaze that, to Millie, seemed mocking. Millie had shunned this cat in the past, had even retreated inside when her spirits were frail. Now, one misty morning, with Morton at work, she glimpsed the cat through the kitchen window, and on an impulse cut a chunk from the steak she meant to cook that evening. She opened the glass-paneled door slowly, and the cat rotated his head with an "It's about time" haughtiness in his eyes. Millie neared the cat like a supplicant and laid the offering on the rail, and withdrew a respectful distance without turning her back. The cat appeared to have done this before, so comfortable was he with the ritualistic deference of a human. He waited poised on his haunches until the time was right, then strolled to the morsel, poked at it as if at a bloodied mouse, then licked the moist red flesh with a sandpaper tongue before bending his sinewy neck over the flesh and sinking his fangs in until it was devoured. Without a glance at his benefactress, the cat sauntered to the edge of the rail and leapt up onto the bare trunk of a tree, caught it with his claws and disappeared into the boughs.

Later that morning Millie purchased a fantasia of lavender, teal, and turquoise scarves in downtown Mill Valley. Alone in the living room before the great window overlooking the hills, she clutched at the thick carpet with her toes, swirled with eyes closed to the rhythm of a Spanish guitar, and twirled the long scarves like a rhythmic gymnast, although she felt awkward and lost her balance at times. She set her jaw and furrowed her brow, became vexed by her tenseness and tried to relax, did relax, and danced for an hour.

Drained and drenched, elevated, lightheaded, she stole into the bedroom and searched her husband's oaken bedside book-chest seeking *Iron John*, for she hoped to dismiss her man's trips to the woods as the comical desperation of a white-collar, middle-aged, "New Age" Marin County cartoon seeking his lost manhood at a campfire drum circle with like-minded dolts. She found not *Iron John* but everything else, scores of books piled high like multicolored treasures, all recently purchased. There were bird- and tree- encyclopedias, books by the New Atheist trinity of Hitchens, Dawkins, and Harris, philosophy books by the pound, outdoor adventure guides, London, Hemingway, Emerson, Plato, Caesar's *Conquest Of Gaul*, *The Voyage of the Beagle*, Twain's *Letters From The Earth*, several dozen more. She examined each cover like a puzzled archaeologist, digging deep through the layers in the hope of finding something on investing, on the financial crisis, on something, anything partaking of the safe, reliable husband she knew well. But when she reached bottom, he had not been found.

She sat on her husband's side of the bed and breathed deep like a safecracker to steady herself, for she had resolved to crack open the books. With resolution she pried open *God Is Not Great*, skimmed a highlighted passage besmirching *The Scriptures*, and dropped the book like Moses' staff turning into a snake. Emerson seemed safe. It was heavily bookmarked, and on one bookmarked page, highlighted in green, was the Arabian proverb: "A fig tree, looking on a fig tree, becometh fruitful." She read on, the bright-green trail left by Morton's highlighter exciting her somehow, the thrill of transgressing tickling memories of the fourth grade and Lillian Fried, the one friend of whom her parents had disapproved, the one who had showed her it all, human anatomy, all of it, in glossy color from multiple angles in her college brother's physiology book. She had shied away from Lillian after that, and her parents had served fudge to celebrate.

She read about witches, the modern kind, pagans who worshiped nature and the female form and danced in the woods, just as she imagined her husband doing wild and mysterious things in the woods with his roughhewn warlock leader. She closed the book thoughtfully, checked *Leviticus* and confirmed her recollection: "A man also or woman that hath a familiar spirit, or that is a wizard, shall surely be put to death: they shall stone them with stones: their blood shall be upon them." She shut the *Bible*, placed it with a mischievous grin in one palm and the book about witches in the other, weighed them as if in a balance, then clapped them together and rubbed them like slabs of wet clay.

She sketched female nudes in a sketchbook she had not used since college, and hid the book beneath the mattress.

She sketched herself in the nude with detached craftsmanship and respect for the contours of a body softened by time.

She drove across the Golden Gate Bridge to the Legion of Honor museum and gazed at the female nudes of Renoir and the Renaissance, admiring their fleshy fullness and their comfort with their abundant flesh. At the edge of her vision a gentleman smiled at her, and she smiled inwardly but did not turn to him.

Morton Vickery waited at home. Taut and tan, legs spread wide, hands on his hips, he surveyed the valleys through the great picture window facing Mount Tam. He was a sea captain, the Colossus of Rhodes, a football coach surveying the field, a general overlooking the battlefield. He heard the door open but did not turn around, but gazed at the sunlight on the Sleeping Lady. She glided towards him as softly as a stream, and he felt her arms vining through the crevices between his elbows and frame, climbing up his back, winding round his neck. He felt her warm breath on the moss of his nape, and fell back into her.

Rear View

The afternoon that he left home for good, Stephen Greenwood knelt on the carpet, clutched the arms of his seven-year-old, and bored into his gaze with eyes as hard and serious as drill bits. Max lolled his head like a narcoleptic until his father's voice found just the right note, then he lifted his face to the man. "Nothing's changing," Stephen claimed with intensity that encouraged and alarmed the boy.

Three years later, a year before Stephen ceased his twice-monthly, three-hour-long roundtrips from San Francisco to the grassy suburb he had fled, he learned from his ex that skinny, vulnerable, prone-to-tears Max was being bullied in school. Enlarged and charged by the urge to protect, Stephen endeavored to teach the boy boxing. "Balance," he said in the seclusion of a stand of trees in the park in which they still spent every other Sunday, punctuating the point with an evangelical thrust of his finger. He had grown his hair long shortly after leaving, and when he bounced on the balls of his feet to demonstrate the art of boxing, his hair swished like a horse's tail across newly-toned shoulders. "You look like a Spartan," said Max with a smile aimed shyly at his father's chin. Stephen raised the edges of his plunging mustache and cuffed his son's head affectionately; but to his surprise the boy swatted his hand away and pressed fists to his face, grinning like an elf either magically lethal or powerless and bluffing.

When Max was seventeen—six-foot-two, dough-faced, thin, with hair dyed coal-black and nails to match, and a driver's license and his mother's car—he determined to start seeing his father again. His mother had advised him to forgive his father for his own sake, if not for the sake of his dad; and besides, she added with a shrewd expression, child support would end at eighteen, and wasn't it wise to get in good with your father? Max nodded with respect for his mother's savvy, but his decision was prompted not by financial considerations, but by tales of a city where boys painted their fingernails black.

The man who greeted Max at the door of the studio apartment was not the feral figure of the boy's childhood but a mild presence who shyly lowered his gaze—once penetrating, now uncertain and small—from his son's appraising stare. Uncertain how to greet his son—handshake, soul shake, bro hug, kiss?—Stephen amalgamated them all, and the greeting resembled the grappling of beginning dance partners. An awkward moment later, Stephen held a wooden plaque out to his son with a hopeful gaze—but Max's arms remained limp at his side, and he smiled slyly beneath lidded eyes. "Check it out," Stephen said, a desperate note belying his casual affect. His mustache drooped at Max's bland expression, and a reciprocal smile rose on Max's lips as he enfolded the plaque in long slender fingers. "It's shiny."

Stephen nodded: Friends had warned him about seventeen. "It's shiny, yes. And it has an inscription." He recovered the plaque and gazed at it as if at a prayer book:

To Doc G
For helping us see the beauty of song.
Love, Ms. Kendrick's Klass

A smile bloomed on a father's face. "I had them all singing Beatles songs, Maxim! Fifth graders. Can you imagine?"

"Imagine all the people," Max slurred.

"Lennon reference, that's my boy. I mean man." Stephen squeezed himself down into the workstation between the couch and the small free-standing garage-sale bookcase that divided his living and sleeping areas. "Look at this, Max-A-Million Bucks."

Max looked at the computer screen as directed, but the wordplay drew his gaze back to the years when he was a fresh-out-of-the-box kid whose dad showered nicknames on him like confetti, bandied rhymes and puns like birthday balloons.

Stephen looked up at his son the way a ten-year-old in a go-cart shines up at his parent at the starting line. "It's my YouTube channel, Circus Maximus. For my songs."

"'Twould seem to be." Max's lips parted slightly, like flower petals at dawn.

Mindful of the advice that he not sound critical, Stephen observed, in a carefully calibrated tone: "You've still got that great sardonic—"

"Ironic."

"Attitude, eh?"

"B."

"Har! Hey Maxim, look: Sixty-seven subscribers!"

"Hey, Stephen, look: Some graying hippie wannabe stole your guitar."

Stephen jerked his head back but let the jibe go. "This fan—this *guy's* from Australia."

"He looks twelve. You sure it's legal to even talk with him?"

Uncertain how to read his son's comments or cryptic expressions, Stephen addressed the computer. "This girl—this young woman here—is from England, man."

"They've got Internet there?"

"*Audible sigh.* Listen, dude, are you ready to roll?"

"Sure, dude, if it's French."

"You can't stop that, can you?"

"You can't top that, Shamu!"

"Hey," Stephen said with mock indignation, "I'm not even five pounds overweight." He patted a stomach that was flat from dissolution rather than design. "Let's head to my gig."

"Where I'll dance a jig," Max slurred, his grin shadowing childhood before his dad left.

The café in the Richmond, mere blocks from the sea, was deep and narrow and brightly lit. In the roomy front were thick hardwood tables; in the slender midsection, an upright piano, a scaled-down drum

149

kit, a worn love seat and an upholstered chair; in the back, a cozy nook in which ascetic late-middle-aged scholars read by the table lamps' soft glow. The walls featured black-and-white photos of the neighborhood, and watercolors by neighborhood kids; on the bookcase were dog-eared paperbacks and beaten board games. Stephen held the door open and beamed with a proprietary air at the scene, so much funkier than Starbucks or anything else in his hometown burb—his son's hometown, too. "Cool, is it not?"

"I don't know, is it naught?"

"Dude, you are something."

"In that case, I'm aught."

"*And* you are caught!"

Max arrested his smile as if suddenly conscious that their old rhyming games were painfully unhip, and replaced it with a haughty mask.

"Let's eat," Stephen said, noting the retrenchment.

Though Max slouched like a question mark, he was half a head taller than his dad even so, and gazed at the menu board over his dad's head. "Ummm," he mosquito-droned, "umm umm umm umm... " The counter-girl smiled appreciatively at Max's schtick as well as its discomfiting effect on his dad. "A bowl of *Our Famous Onion Soup*," Max announced at last, "and a big cuppa joe."

Stephen raised his brow. "You drink coffee?"

"Extra large," Max told the girl with a thrust of his chin. She wore the signature adornments of her generation, nose ring and tattoo (red roses with green vines climbing up the throat), but was cool with the dinos of Stephen's generation who sat in the café like magpies all day and all night. Stephen wondered whether his son liked the girl, or liked girls at all: his nail polish and soft skinny frame and languid demeanor suggested gayness to Stephen, who, even after ten years in town, was unsure of the code.

"And a glass of red," Max slurred into the graying hair that thatched his dad's ear.

Stephen smiled at the jest, but Max stared earnestly into his eyes.

150

No jest. With a confidential hush Stephen said, "I'll let you have a sip of mine, old pal. A little sip couldn't hurt, right?"

"No it couldn't, old boy."

As soon as they sat, Stephen raised his wineglass in salute to his son, but Max curled long fingers around his dad's hand in the manner of a Golden Age film star cupping a leading man's hand for a light, and deftly maneuvered the glass to his lips and drank long and hard. Stephen widened his eyes, and Max laughed with husky derision at his consternation. "You're blowing your image, man, getting all excited like a square from the burbs." Max had recently blown past his squeaky-voiced stage and had a deep baritone that he loved to show off.

"Raising your son right, I see!" rasped Ruddy Rod into Steven's ear. The man was in the midst of a six-week coke binge, and unruly tendrils of coke-white hair reached out from beneath his black bowler like vines seeking light. Rod had lately quit the last of the scores of short-term gigs that had comprised his working life, and lived on a crafty disability claim and the proceeds from selling grass around the corner.

"No," Stephen said. "I mean yes, he's my son. But as for raising him right—"

"Horseshit," said Max, with a glance at Rod's encouraging grin. "You're raising me fine," he said, his words belied by the mockery in his smile at Rod.

Rod's protuberant eyebrows—twin snow banks with antennae— quivered at the discord between father and son, and he fixed his shining eyes on Max as if to imply that a bond more potent than that between Max and his father existed between Max and himself. "Your father talks a lot about you," he suggested with a provocative grin.

Max lowered his eyes and smiled demurely.

"And I've written about him, too," Stephen hastened. "You'll hear that tonight."

Rod leaned in on Max like a barfly imposing wisdom by force of will tinged with menace. "And they're *good*," he intoned, pressing Max's slender forearm to the table, and squeezing as if to test Max's will.

Put on guard, Max told the table: "I can't wait to hear 'em. He used to sing me to sleep in the old days. Solid gold days," this last with a private smile at his dad. The smile was like those he would discreetly share with Stephen at age seven to proclaim his allegiance when Mona would deride Stephen's constant talk about moving to San Francisco in order, Stephen said, to plug into music, meet colorful people, discover himself. Stephen thought he recognized the supportive expression but wasn't quite sure, for he had removed his glasses in anticipation of the show. Before he could make sure, Rod leaned in between the two.

"Man, your kid looks like Lincecum, with that gorgeous long hair. And that wise-guy grin, too, like he knows something special we're too old, or too screwed up, or too old *and* screwed up to get. Didja get him his *Let Timmy Smoke* tee yet, or are you gonna plead poverty like always?"

"I didn't get it, and I'm not planning—"

"You're not?!" Rod said with a preposterous show of fake astonishment. He straightened up and burlesqued perfect posture, and tapped his nose to show Stephen he understood his role. "Of course you're not! Hell no you're not! Don't smoke grass, Maxwell Silver Hammer. Your father is right." To Stephen he added, "I'm going out back to not smoke myself."

Stephen's tone was weighted with doubt and remorse. "I'm not even sure why I hang with that guy, Max. He's a decent drummer and an interesting guy... a real local character, you know? He's not that bad if—"

"Forget it, man. Weed's great."

Stephen felt duty-bound to protest, but the kaleidoscopic changes in his son's countenance puzzled and froze him. "You'll like our songs, Max. At least, I hope you will."

"*I* hope for a thrill!" An impish challenge gleamed in Max's eyes.

Stephen sang to his guitar, Ruddy Rod beat drums and Big Sal thumped bass. They covered three Beatles songs and two Neil Young tunes, and then, with eight folks tuned in with approval, they played

Stephen's songs. Stephen introduced each with an anecdote about the song's origin or moral thrust as Rod twirled his sticks as he grinned at the ceiling and Big Sal held his crescent-moon chin high with the dignity of a palace guard. "This was inspired by my lost dog," Stephen would say. "This is about my Grandma Greenbaum's soulful chicken soup. This is for my father, Major Achievement, who famously told Uncle Steven, speaking of me: 'He's not a pimple on his old man's ass.'" Stephen sang with an aching voice and a seeking stare that clanked against his son's downcast head: Max was texting. He texted throughout. Stephen's voice quivered in response to his son's punching of the keypad, and beads of sweat pushed through the pores of his forehead, flooding him with memories of the day at sixteen when—awkward, zitted, friendless for the most part—he made a public service announcement to a classroom full of mocking kids.

He finished a song and gulped water.

"Max," he entreated, his son's smirking gaze fixed to his phone. "Maxim!" he said with unmeant desperation. Max looked up with the mildly amused gaze of a TV viewer. Stephen gazed helplessly at the cluster of folks engaged with his music in the hope they sympathized. "Maxie," said Stephen, tender and bare. "I wrote this song for you."

Stephen had spent most of the past year learning to play like Neil Young: his optometry gig, part-time by design, gave him time for his music. He played the song well on the Martin he'd saved for two years to buy.

"For you," (he sang to his languorous son)
"to help me sing
what I couldn't say to you,
to find and renew you,
to sing my song loud,
to make my boy proud… "

the guitar's blue-green notes saturating the lyric of a father-son separation and a father's belated quest for redemption. There was an appreciative reduction of chatter as Sal's fat bass notes dropped emotional depth charges and Rod's jazzy brushes softened the palette. Stephen resolved the song with a willowy *for you* as renascent feelings of fatherhood surged through him. Sweet applause from hearts joined in concord lifted his spirits.

"Maybe we forgot to tell y'all, this is a record release party," he said, holding high the CD he had spent eight months recording with a year's worth of savings. "So if you're the sort of person who likes to buy this sort of music, this is the sort of music you might like to buy."

"Or not," said Rod, crashing the cymbal.

"Buy or die," slurred Max.

Stephen stepped to Max's table and ceremoniously handed his CD to him as Rod passed his bowler beneath a scattering of bills that he fluffed like salad greens. Max studied the CD case. "*Seeking Home?*" he said. "You should call it *My Son's Missing Art Lessons*, or whatever."

Stephen froze with his forearm crooked at a right angle to his body. A woman with spiky silver hair who had listened intently to the music clasped Stephen's wrist in a hand whose bones showed like bat wings through baggy skin. "I'll take one," she said with a compassionate twinkle. "That was wonderful."

Stephen accepted her support with evident gratitude and engaged her in a prolonged conversation, for her questions about his songs validated him as an artist. He resolved to mount her ten-dollar bill on a plaque, for this his first record sale. He sold a second CD to the woman's grown daughter, then turned to discover that Max was gone. His CD remained on Max's vacated table.

Stephen walked to his car beneath a moonless sky in which sheets of fog jetted in from the ocean. He settled into his car, which was cold, and inserted his CD. The quality of the music and the intelligence of his lyrics consoled him, as did the knowledge that he had created it all, in a professional manner. And was he not, he mused, a *professional* musician, having just drawn other peoples' hard-earned money from their wallets in exchange for his music? He drove to the corner and rolled a right turn, listening to his music with reviving spirits. Partway down the block he checked the rearview and glimpsed Ruddy Rod, unmistakable for his bowler hat and jangling gait. Rod was flinging his hands up into the air as if tossing confetti over the head of his gangly companion, a tall rubbery form receding from view who seemed to be Stephen's son, Stephen just couldn't tell.

Our World, Your Home

"Welcome back, Mr. Saunders. Your room is waiting." The young woman at the front desk wore a pillbox hat and a snug woolen suit of sea-foam green. The outfit and the woman's cheerful manner suggested a stewardess, but Saunders couldn't recall any airline with a uniform that color. That disturbed him, for he had flown them all. "Here's your key, sir." The woman's smile was as radiant as that of a woman he had known before—or was he thinking of a toothpaste commercial? In any case the smile reassured him, and he leaned across the desk with the confidential sort of smile that had charmed women for years, a smile that implied that life was short, so why not have fun? "It'll be good to take a load off," he grinned. But the woman jerked her gaze down to her notepad, not quickly enough to hide an erupting smile. Saunders sensed that the smile was on him, and his smile sagged and his eyes tightened.

The woman called for the bellhop, and Saunders nodded his consent even though she had not asked for it. Saunders never would have allowed another man to carry his bags in the old days, but he could afford the tip, he told himself with pride. Besides, he reflected, it was wise to acknowledge one's limits, and good for young men like this slovenly bellhop to do physical work.

He was comforted by the familiarity of his room. Except... when had the wallpaper been switched for muddy green, with a hectic pattern in which grotesque eyes were discerned? "The more things change," he said with a sociable chuckle—but the tall, unshaven bellhop, whose uniform had the top several buttons undone, curled his lips derisively and leveled his hand at Saunders' gut, palm up. "Oh," said Saunders with a suavity of manner intended to imply that while he recognized the bellhop's crude menace, he resided miles above the gutter from which it emanated. He peeled bills into the young man's hand. "Go buy yourself some manners," he muttered, and sighed with relief that the youth had not heard. "I'll let you know if I need anything," Saunders called facetiously after as the bellhop swaggered to the door.

Saunders closed the door quickly and inserted the knob of a flimsy looking chain into the slot of the track-plate. With a finger to his lips he examined the screws that secured the chain and the plate. Their heads were exceedingly small, and half were loose. He touched one tentatively; it fell to the floor. He picked it up and studied it with an affect of expertise, and frowned to see that it was a preposterous quarter-inch long. "I'll have to replace that," he said in the manner of a husband speaking aloud to reassure his wife that repairs will be made.

"Home sweet home," he said with a brisk exhalation. He stepped to the window and worked the cords to draw back the heavy drab-green curtains. "I feel like the old man and the sea working the fishing line," he chuckled. The sheer white glass curtain was bright with daylight, and in its center, a few inches above the level of Saunders' head, was a football-sized cockroach drawn in the primitive style of a cave painting. Saunders clutched his chest. "Ho ho," he said, "quite amusing." The thought of a youth defacing the curtain made him coltish. He opened the shuttered door of a tall eight-inch-wide storage closet and rummaged through the clutter. Behind a rusted can of Folgers, a bag of rubber bands, and several ancient little bottles of supermarket spices of forgotten brands, he found a flyswatter. "It's never too late to have a second childhood," he said with spirit, and swatted playfully at the roach, terrified lest the monster skedaddle behind the curtain. "It's so nice to have a man around the house," a familiar female voice said. Saunders smiled with surprise and parted the glass curtains with the flyswatter, then stood with legs wide and arms akimbo to regard the city like a business titan, as he had regarded cities all over the world. A crab's claw of whitewashed buildings five stories tall enveloped the far end of a grand park of dense broadleaf trees and gravel footpaths that converged at strange angles on a central plaza with a great wading pool and a central fountain. Children seated at the edge of the pool thrashed their feet as a woman glided past, performing the breaststroke with long, lithe limbs. She seemed to be naked but Saunders wasn't sure, for her form was obscured by a glassy film of water, and Saunders' vision was impaired by harsh daylight. Saunders bit his lip at the woman's beauty and jerked his gaze to a random patch of grass beneath the trees. In the deep shade, the desk clerk in her sea-foam-green outfit lay on her side facing the insolent bellhop. The bellhop snaked his arm across the woman's waist and drew his fingers down her spine and along the valley of her derrière. She wriggled as the bellhop tugged the zipper on the side of her skirt.

Saunders turned with a gasp from the window.

The fizz of an Alka-Seltzer tablet in water comforted Saunders, and the unpleasant taste made him smile like a good boy who has taken his medicine. "Now for TV," he said, rubbing eager papery palms. It was an old-fashioned remote with push-buttons, and Saunders clicked it like a ray gun. Many wonderful programs were on. "This is your life, Harmon Saunders." Saunders was dimly conscious that the host had not really spoken his name, but that didn't matter, for the respect of coworkers, the love and affection of family and friends—these were universal, and these were his portion. *This Is Your Life* is every man's life.

Saunders was delighted to discover that another favorite show was on, a family saga from the 50s—but his glee was tempered by the realization that he had rarely, if ever, seen an episode all the way through. *Oh well*, he thought, *that's the price of success. And of the first color TV on the block.* This show, too, conveyed universal truths, and Saunders saw himself in the kind father and good husband at the heart of the show. The spirited teen could have been his Russ, and the doting wife, always ready to correct her man's well-intentioned missteps with a gentle jibe, could have been his first wife, Jane—though not his second, Yvette. The three-year-old daughter, climbing from her father's lap up onto the top of his great armchair while he read to her, resembled so closely his own little Susie. Or *Suze*, or *Soo-Soo*, he was sure she'd been called. What books had he read her? Orange flashed in his brain. "How silly," he told the TV-Susie out loud, "to call an *orange* fish a *gold*fish!" There was another daughter on

158

the show too, a vivacious teen, and this girl did not merely resemble Susie, she *was* the teen Susie, with her swishing ponytail, flashing smile, and shining black eyes. And when this girl looked at her TV-father with complete faith in his wisdom and love, Saunders wept with nostalgia.

"Won't you keep it down in there?" The voice on the other side of the wall was disturbed but restrained, like the TV-mother during a crisis. Saunders choked his sobs short and peered as if to penetrate the TV screen. But Susie turned directly to him with eyes full of teen anguish, and Saunders' sobs returned. "Won't you *please* keep it down?" came the voice through the wall, not entirely lacking in tenderness.

Saunders heaved a sigh. "I'd better put this right," he said. "It's what a man does." He stepped from the room and tapped on the next door over. "It's open," came Jane's voice. There on the bed was his three-year-old Susie—or *Soo Soo*, or *Suze*—nestled in Jane's arms. Susie's eyes were fixed on a picture book that her mother held, but her gaze changed from enchanted to annoyed when her mother failed to resume reading. "Won't you please let us read," Jane begged Saunders. Then she added, politely: "I'm sorry you can't join us."

"I wanted to," Saunders said, his face sagging like hot wax.

Jane shrugged philosophically. There was no rancor in melancholy eyes. But Susie looked up. "He doesn't belong here, Mom. Does he?"

"It's too late," Jane told Saunders.

"You're right," Saunders said. "I'm sorry I disturbed you. Obviously I'm in the wrong room." Saunders watched for a reaction, hoping they'd correct him—but Susie had melded with her mother already and the two were inert. Saunders stepped away on stick-insect legs.

In the hallway, Saunders turned the wrong way and walked on spongy carpeting in search of his room. A stampede of teens charged towards him, and his knees buckled as he lunged for the wall, and he pressed himself against the wall like a runner avoiding the bulls at Pamplona. After the teens passed, he smiled with good humor at a handsome young man and a beautiful young woman who had flowed through the teens, but they giggled like a prom king and queen at a nerdy math teacher, then entered their room with champagne in hand. These are not my people, Saunders said. My people are near. They'll invite me in.

Saunders smiled at his prescience when the boisterous voices of several young men bubbled out of a room. He lifted his hand to rap on the door but smiled to remember that Parker Street in Berkeley had an open-door policy that made it a choice destination for students from all over campus. There they were on the couch: Buzz, Ed, and Jeff, smiling up at their friend with wineglasses raised. "Home sweet home," said Saunders in a supple voice, and plopped himself down on the overstuffed brown armchair that he and Jeff had wheeled away from a frat house on a two a.m. dare. Wine was poured. Cigarettes lit. Glasses clinked. Dostoevsky discussed. Cold War policies debated. Adlai Stevenson praised. Bourgeois taste deplored. Saunders closed his eyes and absorbed the conversation with an amiable smile, absorbing as well the jazz that played through the night, and not just Mulligan, Getz, or Chet Baker, but the hard angry bop of Coltrane and Parker. At three a.m., with blissful half-lids, Jeff proposed a trip across the bay to San Francisco, "to prowl the negro streets at dawn." Saunders stifled a scornful giggle at Jeff's affected words, gray sweatshirt, and wispy goatee, but was too honorable to chide his friend. But it bothered him, he had to admit, to contemplate the pretty girl who been sitting silently by Jeff's side all evening, for Jeff was clearly undeserving of such a girl, and she was clearly uncomfortable with Jeff's arm being draped so possessively around her shoulders. How preposterous Jeff's possessiveness was, when he had just nodded in agreement with Buzz's condemnation of middle-class mores. Saunders admired the girl for not openly exhibiting her discontentment with her boyfriend, and complimented himself on averting his gaze from her eyes, which clearly sought his.

Saunders had not felt so happy in years. He was overcome with a delicious tiredness. He arose and issued a general goodnight. Then, on an impulse, he leaned his hand upon Jeff's thigh and kissed him

160

tenderly on the forehead. Oh, those mad college days!

It was a joy to lie in his old college bed, with *Playboy* centerfolds and a Stevenson poster on the wall, and the hum of voices and jazz saxophone lulling him to sleep. His dream was delightful. In a meadow bright with daisies, Jeff's girl, Melody—he recalled the name now— unbuttoned a flower-print blouse and tossed it aside, and laid herself back on the grass with her arms stretched up towards him. He lowered himself and they melded in bliss. But a honking sax awakened Saunders, and he opened distraught eyes. Elation returned, however, when he discovered that Melody was lying next to him, delectable and dreaming. He reached for her waist; but when his palm met her skin she awoke with a howl and recoiled from his touch as if it had burned her. She snatched the bed-sheet and arose with a hiss, wound the sheet around herself and rushed from the room. Saunders followed after on aching knees. Melody collapsed on the floor in a corner while Jeff and the others, dressed nattily for Monterey Jazz, stood facing the doorway from which Saunders emerged.

You did it again, Jeff said with a patient paternalistic smile.

He did, agreed Edward.

He is what he is, Buzz sighed, and the three raised martini glasses overhead and beamed up at their intertwined arms. They called themselves The Triumvirate. What rubbish, thought Saunders.

"I'll just go home now," said Saunders, and crept to the door.

The hallway had an empty morning-after feel. Trays bearing plates of half-eaten room-service food sat outside doorways. Flies buzzed the trays apathetically. The hallway was vacant except for Saunders, who wandered the halls in search of his room until a wailing voice arrested his attention. He tapped on the door.

"Oh, it's you. Come in." Jane's voice was sharp, but the wailing that Saunders had heard was Susie's. She was nine or ten, maybe—he never could peg her appearance to any particular age, having been absent so often as she grew—and she sat shuddering on the edge of the bed with her back to the door. Susie's pain shot through Saunders. It must be that fear of the abyss, he thought, that tormented her after

161

that trip to Disneyland, the Matterhorn ride, with Janie and someone. "I'm here to help," he said in imitation of the gentle key that had made his grandfather so beloved in the family. He drew his lips into a kindly smile that wearied his eyes.

Jane snapped her head back. "Put your money on the table, please."

"Of course," said Saunders. The girl's therapy. How many thousands had he paid through the years? How many fathers would have done that, would have traveled ceaselessly to earn the necessary funds? Congratulating himself, he set his wallet upon the table. "You don't need me here. I can see that." But now Susie was fifteen or sixteen, clad in a frilly dress of wedding-cake white. She rotated her face a quarter turn towards her father, though not far enough to meet his eyes. Her cheekbones were sculpted alabaster. She arose and performed a graceful pirouette, then performed several more which led her out of the room.

Saunders walked the hallways for hours. Each floor rose to the next by means of a winding ramp, and Saunders was grateful that he did not need to climb stairs or crowd himself into an elevator with god-knows-what kind of strangers. He was exhausted by the time he reached his room on the thirty-third floor. The room was dark and empty and smelled of moth balls. Saunders switched on the desk lamp. A thick black leather-bound volume with information for hotel guests sat on the desk, and Saunders smiled at the long-retired slogan of the hotel, inscribed in gold letters:

Welcome Home

"Silly slogan," mused Saunders, who considered the present slogan, in place for decades, more sophisticated:

Our World, Your Home

162

How nice it would be to look down upon the city at night. Saunders stepped to the sliding glass door. "Success has its privileges," he remarked.

But when he stepped out onto the balcony, he felt a void beneath his feet. And when he looked out towards the city, he saw only blackness.

One Good Thing

I had, it seems, a cowboy hat—back in the day, when I was four. I believe that I did. I loved Westerns, and I loved my cap guns—the sulfurous smoke, the thrilling *pop*—so it makes sense that I would have had a cowboy hat, too. I loved that hat, the story goes. I imagine I did. What four-year-old wouldn't? According to family legend, my father came home for dinner one night—"To what do we owe this honor!" was Mom's favorite remark—and ordered me to take my hat off. Which, being a self-respecting cowboy, I refused to do. My father, furious, it is said, snatched the hat off my crew-cut head. And, here's the rub, I reportedly went tromping into the kitchen to tell my mother, in words she loves to quote to this day: "You tell *that man* to give me my hat back!" My mother must have laughed herself silly. Must have, I say, for the use of *That Man* as an epithet for my father quickly became a pet joke that Mom found hilarious and expected me to find funny as well. Maybe I did. I don't recall. What I do recall is trying to mirror Mom's grin, twisted at one end like that of The Joker, every time she referred to "That Man."

Oh, the stories she would share of "That Man!" Such as: "That Man never *once* played catch with you, Tommy!", poking the air as if sticking a dagger through the heart of That Man. "No Tommy, not once!" Not once! Though she'd begged him—"Begged him!"—to play ball with his son, the sunken-eyed kid from the only broken home on the block, whose sole joy in life was baseball (well, and cowboys, of course, as we deduce from The Tale Of The Snatched Cowboy Hat; as well as, if memory serves, playing ditch, tackle football, swimming, scavenging trash in back alleys, climbing trees, wrestling with the dog, and any number of childhood joys that didn't suit the point of the story.)

Yet despite the rich humor, Mom's chief honorific for That Man was *Your Father*, uttered, always, with dark undertones: "Don't expect *Your Father* to (teach you to bike/take us to the park/fix the back fence)." I was so accustomed to hearing "Your Father" that I took that to be That Man's title: "Is *My Father* going to be here at bedtime tonight?" ("*No!*"). Mom took comfort in my custom of referring to my father *as* "My Father" years after my childhood had passed, for it meant I still adhered to her orthodox dogma: Your Father is *bad*. Your Father is *to blame*. Which is why she winced earlier this evening, thirty years after the cowboy-hat tragedy, when I demanded of her, "Mom, please. Tell me one good thing about Dad" (*Dad*), "and I'll leave you alone." The request was not new. I'd tendered variations of the plea several times in the course of my holiday visits in the ten years since Dad's death. What *was* new was that I was a dad now, too—my four-year-old son was playing on the rug with Duplos, tuning out the tension—and I was not going to be denied any longer.

Mom sighed. She touched her chin with a dumpling-like finger, bowed her head from the weight of her sorrow, then raised it with a gargantuan effort and gazed at me with the sad brown eyes that had comforted me all those hot summer nights when I'd hide my head beneath the pillow against the slamming of doors and the tearful shouts of Dad's last years at home. "What do you *want* from me?" she pleaded. I was taken aback. I... didn't know. What did I want? And why must I cause you pain? I, your comfort through those years of strife before my dad left, and your sole consolation through the desolate years afterwards. I, who would have done anything to make you happy, but couldn't.

"Mom, *please*. You got divorced *twenty-five years* ago, and all I'm asking you is to say one good thing about my father."

Her chest heaved beneath her faded nightgown. I feared she would have a heart attack. With showy exasperation she said, "I don't know what to tell you, Tommy."

I looked down at Jack, building a red and green skyscraper on the same floor where I had shared one of the few happy moments with my father that I recalled, an early childhood memory that I have always clung to like a moonbeam. It was a warm summer night, like this one. The gathering dusk was still, and heavy as a curtain. The double door to the patio was open, as now. Dad was rocking in the near darkness—and I was on his lap, in blissful peace. "It *never happened*," Mom had told me once with an air of unshakeable certainty. And why not, Mom? Why *couldn't* it have happened! We had a rocker, and I had a dad—and he lived here until I was eight. Why *couldn't* he have hoisted his five-year-old last-born onto his lap... rocked him in the darkness... stroked his silky brown hair and murmured with delight at the coolness of the sea breeze caressing our brows? "Why *couldn't* it have happened?" I asked—careful, as always, to blunt my tone. She just shook her head and pitifully declared, as if pounding a gavel: "It *just never did*."

But this time I was not backing down. "Alright, Mom, I'll make you a deal. Tell me *one* goddamned good thing about Dad, and I'll drop it forever." Her eyes blackened as they would when I'd dare talk back as a kid—and, like a kid, I still feared her wrath, feared being cast out of her heart like My Father. I lowered my voice to a respectful level. "Listen, Mom, I want you to tell me just one good thing about my father—whose blood is in me as much as yours is, and in your beautiful grandson, too."

She shook her head sadly, made a showy pantomime of searching her memory and coming up empty. She stared at her grown-up boy in need with the sad, loving eyes of lullabies past. "Well," she sighed, her voice softer now, "he made his child-support payments on time."

"Good, Mom. That's a start. A lot of divorced dads don't do that at all."

I'd made too much of it. "Oh, *Thomas*," she said. "He would have been thrown in *jail* if he hadn't."

"*Jesus*, Mom, he wouldn't have been thrown in jail!" I tried another tack. "Look, Mom, you told me once he sold insurance in the black part of town. That was a good thing to do, right? I mean, how many white people had the guts to go into the ghetto to help black people in the Sixties, when there were riots and stuff."

That was nothing, a mere fly to swat. "He sold them insurance they didn't even *need*, Tom."

"What do you mean, didn't need!" My voice was rising like a

teen's, but I just couldn't help it. "Why *didn't* black people need insurance? They had kids and died too, didn't they? Black people need insurance like anyone else!"

"I am *not* going to discuss it, Thomas." She turned as if from a wretch.

"Well I am!" At the sound of my sharp tone, Jack looked up in confusion with maple eyes like his grandma's. "Jacko, could you go give fresh water to Peanut?" I should have sent him out of the room before, but I treasured every second with him. "Well, Mom, I *am* going to discuss it, because I think it was a good thing he did. And what about the B'nai B'rith—he was really active in that, right? And that was a service organization, wasn't it?"

Again the eyes of absolute judgment. "He was in it to make *money*, Thomas."

"Well, sheesh, Mom, everyone has mixed motives. So what if he made business contacts there? That doesn't mean he wasn't also serving the community."

The look on her face said she had me in her sights. From long experience I knew that I could advance a pawn, or sometimes capture a minor piece, but she always had something strong in reserve. "He *stole* the membership list for business purposes, Thomas. People got so fed up with him pestering them at home, they finally had to call Ben Pilcher—and your father was almost thrown out on his ear!"

"What do you mean, *stole* it!" I couldn't believe the whine of my voice. I was trying to push out so much feeling without raising my voice, it sounded like the highest pitch on a sax. "What do you mean, *stole* it? It was just a list of names, how the heck could you *steal* it? And anyway, he was just trying to make a living, right? Just trying to keep a roof over our heads!"

"This was my *mother's* house, Thomas, she gave it to me. Your father had nothing whatsoever to do with it."

"Well, fine, then, he was trying to feed us, okay? I mean, I'm sure some of the money he earned with his hard work found its way into our mouths."

"*Hard work*," Mom spat. She folded her arms and turned away, my point too pathetic to even rebut, confident there was nothing I could throw her way that she couldn't swat down. Then she slowly rotated her head toward me like a turret-mounted big gun. "And he never *once* played catch with you, Thomas. Not *once!*"

"*Alright* already! I've heard it a million times!"

Which did not stop the story. "I told him after he left us, 'David,' I said, 'if you want to get close to Tommy, play catch with the boy. All he lives for is baseball.' But he never made time to play catch with you, Tommy. Not once!"

"*Alright* already! Alright, he never played damned catch with me!"

Or... did he? It seemed to me... yes! Yes he did! He sure as hell did! I don't know why, but the recollection came back to me right then and there as if borne by fairies through the still summer night. Dad *had* played catch with me, once. I was eight, and Dad had moved out about six months before, and the Scouts were having a father-son picnic. I had worried all week, because it looked like Dad wasn't going to take me because he and Mom had just had a big fight, and my big brother Mike would take me instead. But when Sunday arrived, Dad was there to take me. He picked me up in his new Caddie, the one Mom yelled at him for buying. That car was a sight, with those long stylish fins, all that gleaming chrome, and its Cape Ivory coat, all stretched out in the middle of the street like a yacht.

Of course it was the middle of the street, Dad always waited in the middle of the street in front of our house when he picked us three kids up for our Sunday visits. And when he blew the horn, it always sounded angry. One time he had come to the door, and Mom hollered at him and threatened to call Dave Jaffe, a bogeyman also known as "The Lawyer." So he'd blow the horn and out we'd march, my older brother, older sister and me, and we'd ride to a coffee shop where Dad would embarrass us by showing us off to the waitresses. "How do you like these kids of mine?" he'd beam. The waitress would look us over and pronounce us "precious." Then she'd sashay away while Dad stared after. "What a sweetheart," he'd say. Then we'd settle in and talk about, I don't know what. There must have been something. My older brother, the firstborn and seven years older than me, had a rapport with Dad, and they had genuine multi-word exchanges that sounded like conversation. My sister, eleven, would poke at her eggs with her fork. She always ordered eggs over easy, and always left the yolks—actually, she left almost everything. I found out later that Mom sent her to a shrink to help her start eating again after the divorce. Dad would reach across the table and fork a yolk from her plate and plunge it whole into his mouth. This was fascinating and repulsive, something only a grownup would do.

After breakfast, we'd push on to miniature golf or bowling. Dad had taken up bowling after the divorce, and he'd bought a glossy blue ball with his initials engraved: "D.A.D.," for David Aaron Davis. I thought it was cool that Dad's ball said "DAD," but Mom pointed out that it had nothing to do with fatherhood: "Nothing whatsoever." A few times, right after the divorce, Dad took us bowling with a woman who also owned her own ball. She wore clingy pullovers and slacks, and was slender—unlike Mom—and pretty in a waxen way. She smiled at us kids when she was introduced to us, then spent the rest of the day smiling at Dad in an intimate way. Then she suddenly stopped coming, and we started bowling with the B'Nai B'rith, a Jewish service organization.

"Watch," Dad told me on one of these occasions in his two-pack-a-day rasp, "here's how you line up a shot. You don't aim for the pins, you aim at this arrow."

The ball was so heavy I could hardly lift it, let alone aim it.

"Now step like this." He pantomimed the rhythm of the approach without the ball while I stood there conscious of his cronies scrutinizing me. I knew I could never roll the ball straight. "Now watch this," Dad said, and glided down the lane and swung his arm free, and down the pins went. His average was 190. Mine was 32.

"Now you try."

It went straight in the gutter.

Irritated, he snapped: "Not *that* way, Moshe, aim for the arrow!"

My name wasn't Moshe, it was Tommy. Mike, my older brother, was *Moshe,* and that was only on Sundays, when we were with the Jews. "I mean, Tommy."

My lip quivered.

"Oh for Chrissake, *now* what's the problem?" The rasp was harsher. Dad hated it when I'd get upset.

"Dad, I don't want to play bowling."

"I've already paid for the god-damned games!" Then he realized he was shouting, and looked around red-faced to see if his lodge brothers or whatever were watching. "I've paid for the god-damned games already." It was odd to hear "god-damned" in a hushed voice.

"But I don't wanna play." My voice was all wiggly.

He knelt to me and exhaled smoke, a nauseating smell. "Oh what's wrong, Tommy?" His eyes were as black and hard as cannonballs. He gripped my arms, but I shrugged his hands off. He rose up above me like the demon towering up over Bald Mountain in *Fantasia.* "You know what your problem is, Tommy? You're too god-damned sensitive!"

And the tear-storm came. Mike stepped between us and convinced Dad to forget about me, and I sat with my sister while Mike and Dad bowled. The same scene played out, Sunday after Sunday.

But I liked the Cub Scouts, for I liked being around boys and their dads—especially after my dad moved out. And the day Dad took me to the Father-Son Picnic was so different from all the other Sunday visits. This time it was just him and me, and I got to ride up front. I felt so good I even risked his annoyance by pushing the buttons on the radio; but he just puffed on his cigarette, smoke after smoke—though the smoke made me sick—all the way to the park. Dad rolled past the ball fields and golf course to the artificial lake where model boats sailed, and pulled the Caddie into the lot like a cruise ship docking. He had just had it washed and waxed that morning, and its coat shone and its chrome gleamed. Kids in my Scout den were wrestling on the grass in their blue uniforms, and their dads were there, too, hearty Jewish men with strong, hairy arms: Mr. Schumpler, the butcher, with arms (it's a fact) thick as hams; Mr. Perl, the plumber, whose son, Stevie, won the soap-box derby—with lots of help from his dad, we suspected; Mr. Picus, the grocer, whose son Morty stocked the shelves after school; and Mr. Katz, the lawyer, whose son could name the U.S. presidents in reverse order and spit farther than anyone in the den.

As we walked across the rolling lawn I still felt nauseous from the cigarette smoke in the car. I was anxious, too, for I hadn't been in the den for very long and wasn't close with the guys, and I didn't know how my dad would act. I looked up at Dad, and he looked anxious, too. This surprised me, since he was always the loudest, most gregarious man at his B'Nai B'rith gatherings. He always told us kids that confidence—"You need more confidence, Tommy!"—was the reason he had been named Top Producer in his insurance company two years running. I remember staring at the Top Producer plaques on the wall of his apartment and wondering what a Top Producer was. Dad stared at me as I stared at the plaques, but for some reason, I couldn't get excited. "Can we go now?" I said. He snorted, and we rode home in silence.

The guys in my den were wrestling in twos and threes, a rolling shrieking mass. I hung around the periphery with a hopeful half-grin, then Bobby Picus shoved me into the shoving, pushing, laughing mix. We interlocked like Lincoln Logs until no one could move, and quivered with such hilarity that we looked like a giant blue gelatin mold. That's all it took for us kids to get grooving.

For the dads it was different. They gathered around the grill and stood kind of sideways to each other as they spoke, glancing at us, or the grill, but seldom at each other. My dad stood at the edge of the group. Mr. Schumpler had brought fresh-ground hamburger patties from his butcher shop, and stood over the grill sprinkling them with salt and pepper while the other dads nodded as if they were visiting physicians watching a heart surgeon performing a particularly difficult operation. When it was time to eat, every kid sat next to his dad at a long table where we ate burgers and chips and watermelon and Jell-O. Then Mr. Katz, the den leader, suggested a father-son softball game, which I was for. I wasn't especially good at softball, but I loved the game, and it made me feel secure in social situations because I knew what to do, and did not have to talk. Dad felt different. "Why don't we just let the kids play," he told the other dads. "Us old guys ought to rest in the shade." His air was humorous, but he was faintly desperate. It was true that he didn't want to play, but the "old guy" part was silly: he was lean and spry despite his smoker's cough and graying temples.

"What's wrong, Davis?" Mr. Schumpler said, sounding as if he was choking on meat. "Afraid you can't cut the mustard?"

"Oh, I can cut it, you old blowhard. It's just such a waste of a beautiful day."

Mr. Schumpler snorted, and Mr. Katz and his son laid out a makeshift diamond with magazines for bases and a crushed soda can for the pitcher's mound. There were bare patches on the grass from the summer heat, but who cared? We were playing softball, and that was great. I can't remember who won, but we boys played real hard, and the dads clowned around and laughed at their efforts, which were inept in some cases—and the more inept, the more they laughed. Which amazed me. Mr. Katz struck out—how a grown man could strike out in slow-pitch softball was a mystery to me—and made a big show of removing his straw hat and bowing deeply to everyone on the field, to everyone's amusement.

Dad wasn't like that. He swung super hard but only managed to graze the ball, sending it weakly into the infield. He ran hell bent for first and they threw him out—and to make matters worse, he twisted his ankle in a divot, and hopped around yelling "Son of a bitch!" This embarrassed me but thrilled me somehow. Mr. Katz helped Dad over to the picnic table, propped Dad's leg up on a cooler, filled a plastic bag with ice cubes and set it on Dad's ankle.

"Hey, Davis," yelled Mr. Schumpler, "how do you like your seat!" I peeked at Dad, who for once in his life was at a loss for words.

"Give me your glove, Tommy," he said with urgency in his harsh smoker's voice.

So I gave Dad my glove. He stared at it as if it were an alien life form before putting it on. "Is this how you wear it?"

I nodded. "Some guys stick their finger out that hole."

As Dad sat on the bench, with his ankle elevated, I tossed the ball underhanded. He caught it in a funny way. Instead of catching the ball with the glove and clamping his free hand onto it, he'd clap both hands together like a percussionist crashing cymbals. "Again," he'd say, and he'd stare at the softball with the intensity of a safecracker as it sailed towards him. "I'll play now," he said, throwing the improvised ice pack onto the grass with disdain and hobbling towards the field. The other dads made a big show of fawning over him, oohing and aahing with sarcasm-tinged admiration for his bravery. They let him play first, and every time they threw the ball to him, he'd slap his hands together in the manner he had just improvised. Sometimes he'd catch it, and sometimes he wouldn't, and when he wouldn't, he'd hobble after the balls. And the wisecracks stopped.

"How's your ankle, Dad?" I asked as we walked back to the car. My question was dumb, for he was limping badly. He stopped short.

"Listen, Tommy. When I was a kid, we were too busy working our tails off to have fancy picnics and Cub Scout uniforms, and we sure as hell didn't have time for baseball." He stood there like an actor, waiting for me to speak. But I had no idea what line I should say.

"Dad," I said, "are we gonna play bowling next week?" He kind of snorted, then tousled my hair. Then led me limping to the car.

I looked at my mother. Yes, Mom, it happened. That Man did play catch with me once.

Mom looked so old and broken. Her face was so sallow, the lines around her eyes carved so deeply by tears. What's the point? I thought. "Hey, Jacko!" I yelled, and my little Jack came running, his maple eyes gleaming. "Let's go out in the yard," I said. I hoisted Jack up onto my shoulders, and we left the room in which My Father never rocked me—"Not once!"—and walked into the yard. It was dark, and the temperature was so fine that the air felt like an extra silken layer of skin. I walked over to the massive jacaranda tree I had climbed as a kid and lowered Jack to the ground. There was a lawn chair underneath the tree, and I sat down on it and patted my legs. Jack reached up, and I helped him onto my lap and turned him around so that his back pressed against my belly. I wrapped my arms around him and we sat there in silence, gazing at the stars and listening to the crickets. I lowered my face to kiss his hair, but just then Peanut, the dachshund, came scampering out. Jack jumped down with a shout and clomped after Peanut and chased her into a dark corner where they vanished from sight.

About the Author

JON SINDELL is the author of the flash-fiction collection *The Roadkill Collection* and the novel *The Mighty Roman Baseball Blast*. He lives in San Francisco with his wife and near his grown kids. Visit his website at jonsindell.com.

www.ingramcontent.com/pod-product-compliance
Lightning Source LLC
Chambersburg PA
CBHW070025260626
47159CB00005B/1956